S0-BOF-854

Dugan Peckles Through the Manhole

Happy Adventures

Sly Pepper

Sly

MindMaze
Publishing Co.

Dugan Peckles Through the Manhole

by Sly Pepper

MINDMAZE PUBLISHING COMPANY, WOODBURY

This book is a work of fiction. Names, places and characters are "Sly" fantasies.

Dugan Peckles Through The Manhole
Published by MindMaze Publishing Co.

©2004 by Sly Pepper

Art by Dawn Edwards.
Design by Barbara Keith.

ALL RIGHTS RESERVED

No part of this publication may be reproduced, stored in a retrieval system, or transmitted in any form or by any means-electronic, mechanical, photocopying, recording or otherwise without prior written permission.

For information:
MindMaze Publishing Co.
PO Box 251278
Woodbury, MN 55125
duganpeckles.com

ISBN : 0-9747668-0-1
Library of Congress Control Number: 2004101583

Printed in the USA

Dedicated to

Imagination
Courage
Persistance

Live the Magic
Dare the Adventure

CONTENTS

Chapter One

Trouble Again

The grip on Dugan's arm was like rawhide drying in the sun. It grew tighter as each footstep tromped upon the sidewalk. He sneaked a side-glance at Mrs. Murphy, who was still red with anger. Her lips pursed and wrinkles ran across her forehead like worm trails through mud. He had always suspected she was half Comanche. Now he knew. No one but a mighty tracker could have crept up on him and taken him captive like that.

He wished she lived in the next town or the

next state or even Mexico, so that by the time they walked to his house she would forget how angry she was. But they were already charging through his own gate and up the stairs to his greatest dread. He gulped. Why couldn't she just bury him in an anthill, chain him in the dungeon, or send him into the universe on a mission of certain death? No, that wasn't dire enough for her. She was crafty. She knew the worst kind of torture.

As Mrs. Murphy reached for the doorbell, he could already see the look that would come over his mother's pretty face before a single word was said, that angry, sad, desperate, what shall I do with you look, like when he had mixed a magic potion out of her best perfume or made the girl next door kiss a frog.

Then the door opened and his mother appeared in her pink-checkered apron, her mousy hair a bit mussed. There was a dab of flour on her cheek. It was his favorite look, a plain mom baking cookies look. Then her cheerful smile melted like chocolate chips on a hot sidewalk and curled down like old apple peels the moment she saw Mrs. Murphy's he-man grip on Dugan's arm.

His heart dropped into a pothole somewhere behind his stomach, which suddenly didn't feel so good. His mother's brown eyes rested on his face, soft as a peach blossom, devastating as a Samurai warrior.

Mrs. Murphy glared at him.

"Doesn't he belong in school?" she said.

"There wasn't any school today," his mother said.

"I didn't know reform school gave days off!" Mrs. Murphy snapped and her forehead scrunched over narrow, scowling eyes.

"What did he do this time?" Mrs. Peckles asked.

"I spent hours scraping and painting my picnic table," said Mrs. Murphy, "and this -

this - this child turned the sprinklers on it. Do you know what sprinklers do to wet paint?"

Mrs. Peckles stammered with embarrassment and exasperation.

"Dugan, why did you do that?" she asked.

"I didn't know the paint was wet. I was tracking a tiger through the rain forest and I needed some rain," he said.

"But Dugan, you weren't supposed to leave your own yard," his mother scolded.

"The tiger didn't know that," Dugan said. "He was sneaking down the street to eat Mrs. Cobb's rabbit. I couldn't let him eat the rabbit. It's Mrs. Cobb's favorite."

Mrs. Peckles hung her head and closed her eyes. For a moment Dugan thought she was going to cry.

"I'm sorry, Mrs. Murphy. I will speak to my husband and we will fix the table. Is there anything else I can do?"

"You can keep this child on a short leash

where he can't terrorize the neighborhood anymore," Mrs. Murphy snapped, then turned and stomped away.

Dugan slowly followed his mother into the usually cheery house. But now he had stepped into the bowels of the castle where chains rattled and gloom hung like dusty cobwebs. He might never see the light of day again.

"I'm at my wits end," his mother said. "You know you weren't supposed to leave your own yard. How many times have I told you that?"

His bottom lip slid out in dismay as he fidgeted under her stern gaze.

"I won't leave my yard again, Mom. I promise," he said.

"You promised me that already today, and yesterday and last week," she said. "Your promises are no good. You'll have to go to your room until I decide what to do about this problem. And speaking of your room, let's have a look at it."

His heart was already so low he could have stepped on it. The last thing he needed now was for her to see his room. He raced ahead of her up two flights of stairs to his third floor bedroom, and frantically began to gather up the pile of clothes he had thrown out of his bureau drawers onto his unmade bed. Then he stepped on half a peanut butter sandwich he had dropped while looking for his favorite hat.

"A pigpen!" his mother said when she arrived all too quickly. "An absolute pigpen!"

"I can clean it up in a minute," he said and began to pitch toys into his closet.

"A bulldozer couldn't clean up this place. It looks like a dump truck backed in and unloaded."

Then she spied his wastebasket long past due for dumping and picked it up for closer examination.

"Two apple cores, a chunk of rotten banana, and I'm not sure what the other brown glob is," she said. "How many times have I told you this can is not for garbage? It draws ants and I wouldn't be surprised if there was a rat's nest under your bed."

Very cautiously, Dugan raised the bedspread and peeked under it. With everything there was under the bed he couldn't be sure there weren't any rats but at least nothing moved at the moment.

When he straightened up and found his mother still staring at him, he pulled off his safari hat with its big scarlet plume. His sandy blond hair scattered in unruly strands over his blue-green eyes as he peered out at the disappointment on his mother's face. Then he dropped his head and stared at his sneakers. His tanned cheeks flushed and there was a big ache in his small chest. He didn't mean to make his mother angry. She was the greatest mom in town and maybe even as far as Mars or the Milky Way. She understood snorkels in bathtubs, rocks under beds, frog collections, and the importance of milk and cookies after fighting dragons. But even after reading him twenty thousand adventure stories, she still didn't understand that a hero could not stay in his own yard when there were trails to follow or deeds to be done. He thought time would forever stand still in this moment of bewilderment. At last she moved toward the door, then paused with the worst of all words.

"I will discuss this with your father," she said. "Until then, you stay here in your room and clean up this mess."

She closed the door behind her and left him alone. He stood for a moment and listened to her faint footsteps upon the carpeted hall as she moved away from his room. Wasn't that the way it was, just when a hero thought his gallant deeds would be rewarded with cheering crowds of grateful admirers, a troll crawled out into his path and sucked him down into a dark hole beneath a dank old bridge. He sighed and picked up the socks he had worn yesterday and stuffed them back into his bureau drawer. They were good enough for at least one more day. Then he slouched over to his window and leaned on the sill.

A bit of a breeze came in through the screen, soft and warm, carrying the scent of fall leaves. The world outside had a mellow golden glow.

"What a crummy deal. Stuck in my room," he said out loud. "I should be outside on a beautiful day like this. Kids need a lot of sunshine."

He caught a glimpse of the little girl next door. She was pushing her doll buggy around in her backyard. He wished it were he she was talking to instead of her old rubber doll. She moved out of his view and he pushed his face harder against the screen to see where she went.

Then he heard the quick, quiet rip as the screen tore out of its frame. It was a very soft sound, like the kerchoo of a kitten or the paw step of a puppy, but it was the sort of sound a mom could hear from three doors down with the vacuum cleaner running.

He caught his breath and waited with both eyes glued to the door, but his mother did not appear. He sighed with relief, and then tried to push the screen back into place. Instead, the short slit suddenly burst into a long gaping hole. He stared at it as though sheer will could create the magic he needed, but the hole didn't get any smaller. It sure wasn't going to disappear. After a few moments of thought, he decided the only thing left to do was pull the whole screen from the window frame and repair it on the floor.

He headed for his closet where he had placed his latest treasure, his Man-of- Adventure Tool Belt, which his father had designed and made just for him. A wisp of a smile crept upon his face as he thought about his dad.

He was the perfect husband for Melissa Peckles who loved to tell everyone how amazing he was. Someday the whole universe would know the name of Morgan Peckles. Dugan inhaled deeply. "Merlin, Disney and Morgan Peckles," he thought. His chest swelled in contemplation of certain fame.

When Morgan Peckles wasn't sourcing the Internet for his import-export business, he was blissfully engrossed in one of his new inventions. Dugan sometimes received the benefit of this wizardly imagination. Dugan's grin grew broader. Someday he would work alongside his dad, Peckles and Peckles, Techno Conjurers Extraordinaire.

Then Dugan remembered his current mission and carried the tool belt to the window. Now he saw the torn screen as a chance to do a good deed and to use his nifty tool set. He pulled the clips that held the screen in place, and then tugged on the frame. It didn't budge. He tugged again. It still didn't budge. Apparently it was not going to be as easy to get it out as he'd imagined. He wrestled and tugged again. Suddenly it gave way and he tumbled backward onto the floor pulling the screen down upon him. The metal frame kinked and bent. Dugan stared. Wow! This would really take a good deed to fix. He rolled over and placed the screen on the floor.

When he stood up, he sincerely meant to choose a tool and begin the repair but the gaping window caught his attention, first. In a second he had climbed out through the window and onto the flat roof of the second level veranda.

The little girl next door had gone inside while he had been occupied in his own room. But now there was so much more to see. This was a magnificent lookout tower. From here he could see his kingdom. He could see passing cars and boys on bicycles and Bert Fliver four houses down helping his sister put on her roller skates. There was a dog digging a hole and Mr. Thornton kicking his leaf blower across the flowerbeds he was supposed to be cleaning.

Best of all, beyond the acres of corn at the

edge of town, Dugan could see an orange utility truck parked on an old road that ran out into the countryside. He loved utility trucks loaded with tools and ladders and flashing lights. How grand it would be to ride up in a hydraulic lift that could take him to the tops of trees and poles and halfway up buildings. That would take a brave man, but Dugan was brave.

He didn't see any poles or buildings anywhere near this truck. The field of corn hid whatever it was that occupied the workmen. He wondered what they were doing. He pondered on the question for some time, then unable to satisfy his curiosity, his attention turned to the big box elder tree that grew several feet from one end of the roof. Its large branches reached out in all directions. One stout branch swooped right over the porch roof and gave Dugan a wonderful idea.

He ducked back into his room, grabbed his utility belt and strapped it on over his tan jacket with a grand array of pockets and compartments that held important supplies. His mother had sewn it according to his father's design. Upon the utility belt hung a wooden sword, a penknife, a waterproof flashlight, a first aid kit and a collection of other tools and necessities for the adventurous hero. The world was his to claim and with his belt and jacket he would forever be prepared to do so. He plopped his safari hat upon his head. In the mirror he saw a courageous adventurer about to embark upon another mission.

He snatched up the small stool he used for reaching his closet shelf and the top bureau drawer, and set it out the window. The branch hanging over the porch was above his head, but with his stool he managed to pull himself up and straddle it. It made a fine horse.

He raised his sword and called, "Away steed. Dugan the Daring will save the kingdom!"

The branch bounced beneath him as he rode through the enchanted forest of his mind. Then he spied a dragon, and the dragon spied Dugan. It must have known the knight's reputation because it sneaked down a mountainside and tried to hide in its den. Dugan peered over the edge of the roof.

"You can't hide from me, dragon," he called. "I'm not afraid to follow you into your lair. I have my laser beam to light my way and my sword to cut off your head."

He wrapped his arms around the branch and slid out to the tree trunk. There was another branch on the other side. It was a little bit lower. Dugan hugged the tree tightly and stretched his leg down to reach it, but his foot tapped the air. The branch was lower than he had anticipated. He clung to the tree for a moment, and then decided that he had better go back up.

As he looked up, his upper foot slipped and slid off the branch. Dugan dropped. His heart leaped up his throat and his breath stuck like a giant wad of gum on top of it. He thought he was a goner. Then the lower branch he had tried to reach caught his dangling foot and he lodged against the tree.

He glanced down and immediately regretted he had ventured out without first thinking over his course of action. Didn't Dad always say, "Think more, fix less?" Dad would not like fixing this and Mom would like it less. She hated high places. He looked up and knew he could not climb back to the porch roof. He looked down and down and down. Oh, boy! If he called Mom now, she would nail his window and his door shut forever! He hugged the tree tightly and said a little prayer.

"Guardian Angel, I know I bug you a lot. Mom says you have to be the busiest angel in Heaven, but I really need some help!"

He hoped she wasn't as exasperated with him as his mom was. Then he remembered his manners and added "please."

He took a deep breath. His only way out of

the tree was down the tree. He glanced to the next branch. It was only a little ways.

"I'm Dugan the Daring," he said. "Me and Robin Hood rule the forest."

He stretched until he felt the branch, and then lowered himself onto it. As he shifted his hand, his hat slid over his eyes and gave him a momentary scare. But he found his handhold and then tipped his head to let the hat fall. He watched it bounce from limb to limb until it hit the ground. He gulped and paused for a moment.

"The only way to lick fear is to bite it on the nose," Dad always said. Huddling in fear wouldn't get him down to safety. Dugan had to be brave. Morgan Peckles was brave. Knights were brave. Space walkers were brave. He took a deep breath and lowered himself cautiously down to the next limb. And then the next. Branch by branch, he worked his way down the tree. He doubted that even Jack's beanstalk was as tall as this tree. But he was even braver than Jack.

At last he was seated upon the lowest limb. Since heroes always have the luck of the brave, the Peckles' picnic table was nicely positioned beneath Dugan's perch. He slid onto his belly, swung down and dropped onto the table.

From his position of solid footing, he looked back up to where he had started and knew he did not want to try that again, at least not for a few years. Then his daring rekindled and he looked slyly around.

"You thought only a dragon could get down here, didn't you, dragon," he said, and began his game again. "But Dugan the Daring can go anywhere a dragon can go and some places it can't."

He leaped off the picnic table and darted around the grape arbor. Then a mighty battle ensued. Flames bolted like lightening, but he ducked behind the scorch shield his mother sometimes called a barbecue. The moment the dragon drew a breath, Dugan bounded forward, slashing mightily with his sword.

Dragon blood and scales rained around him. With one hand he cleared his vision and with the other he lunged with the fatal stroke.

The ferocious beast was no match for a warrior who could survive the perilous descent down the rocky face of the lookout tower. Dugan felt the rush of conquest. The evil beast lay dead at his feet. He peered around to make certain no others lurked behind the rose bushes or the garbage can. But it was only a one-dragon cave, so he sheathed his sword and with a victor's flourish plunked his hat upon his head.

He knew he should go back up to his room before Mom missed him so he headed for the back door and hoped she was too busy to see him slip up to his room. But half way to the door, he remembered the orange utility truck. He wondered what the workmen were doing out there. He thought for a second. As long as he was already outside, it would only take a few minutes to run across the cornfield and have a look. He couldn't get into trouble out there. No one would even see him amidst the tall corn. He darted out the back gate.

By the time he made his way through the long rows to the other side, the men and truck were gone. He crept out of the corn to the edge of the road and looked around. In the middle of the road gaped a round hole. Beside it lay the manhole cover the men had forgotten to replace.

There's no telling what might be down there, Dugan thought. Since there was no traffic in sight on the lazy country road, he slipped out of hiding and approached the hole. There he stretched out on his belly and peered down into the dark. He thought he heard the trickle of water, but couldn't see a thing. He was, of course, prepared with his ever handy Man of Adventure Belt.

He sat up to unhook the light from his belt, but before he could unclip it, a worrisome buzz began behind his head. He sprang to his feet and spun around. A pair of yellow jackets looped overhead. They swooped so close to his face, he could nearly feel the fan of their wings against his cheeks. He had been stung only a month before and the pain of the experience was still sharp in his mind.

The terrible twosome had just begun their mischief. They sailed by on another run. Dugan waved his hat and danced from side to side. He swatted and yelped, but the wasps would not leave him. They tightened the circle around his head as though they wanted to play in the sandy wisps of his hair.

"Get away!" he shouted. "Leave me alone."

He ducked and batted, then leaped backwards. Suddenly the buzz was gone. There was nothing beneath his feet. The light of day vanished. Only the moment before he hit bottom with a splash and his head bounced off something hard, did he remember the hole that had caught his curiosity.

Chapter Two

Lost

Dugan awoke in total darkness. His head lay upon a bed of gravel. His body lay in a shallow stream of water. He shivered and tried to remember where he was.

When he tried to stand, his head felt as though he had blown up too many balloons. He put his hand on a throbbing ache at the back of his head and felt a sticky, damp bump. His eyes widened in fear. Was his head broken?

"Mother!" he shouted long and pleadingly.

"Mother... mother... mother," the echo taunted.

It was so dark, so very dark. Where could he be? The only sound to break the silence was the trickle of water. He began to sob. With each tearful jerk, the ache sharpened and the bump thumped harder.

Finally he tightened his lips and held his breath in a gallant effort to control the fear and the pain. Then he remembered seeing a man on television who forgot his name when he bumped his head.

"I'm Dugan," he said. "Dugan the Daring. I can go anywhere a dragon can go and some places it can't."

Suddenly he stopped and listened, for he was not at all sure which this was. He fumbled along his belt and found the broken remains of his sword, a jagged half blade upon a handle. His flashlight hung next to it. His small fingers trembled as he unhooked the light and held it in front of him. He was almost afraid to push the switch. What would he do if it failed to light?

An instant later the dread vanished with a burst of light. But the sight was little comfort. He was in a tunnel twice his own height. The ceilings and walls were dirt and gravel. The floor was a slow moving stream of water except for the small patch of gravel he had settled upon. Scraps of paper and waste occasionally drifted by, washed down through the storm drains. Where they had entered was a mystery. Nowhere could he see a hole of even the tiniest size where the sun shined through from the outside.

Again he called the magic word that cured chicken pox, untied knots, chased spooks from the dark and repaired broken ray guns.

"Mother!"

"Mother... mother... mother," the echo taunted. The bump made him feel tired and he fell asleep on the gravel, calling again and again as he drifted off. For the first time in his short life, no one came to scold or mend or kiss away the tears. For what seemed like hours, he alternated sleeping and crying for help.

At last the ache and dizziness lessened and his thoughts cleared. As he pondered his predicament the full realization came to him that he was alone and on a frightening adventure for real. He rose to his feet and shined his light in both directions. Since neither way showed any promise of escape, he set off upstream the way from which he thought he must have floated down. The hole he had fallen through could not be very far away, he decided. But when he shined his light down the tunnel, it disappeared into the darkness. He drew what was left of his sword and held it ready at his side.

He had not gone far before something reached up from the ooze and snagged his leg. He jumped, and then hurriedly shined the light on his attacker. It was only a small branch. Another sign, he hoped, that the hole to the outside was not far away.

As he walked along, he occupied himself with thoughts of his mom and dad. They would soon be looking for him. His heart lightened, then sank again. They would look a hundred thousand places for him. They would look everyplace in town. They would look everyplace except the sewer.

The sewer! Panic bounced his woozy mind. That was where rats lived! Rats as big as cats! With long slinky tails and big sharp teeth and fast little legs that could climb up anything, including a small boy's leg. He shuttered and hastily searched around him with his light. Dragons he could handle, but even knights, cowboys and space walkers did not fool with rats.

He waded forward more cautiously. He listened to the slush of his own steps and for any other sounds that might break the silence. He shivered from what seemed like hours of being wet. His stomach grumbled at its emptiness. He thought about the cookies his mother had been baking and milk and peanut butter sandwiches and all the good tastes and smells that came out of his mother's kitchen. Boy, did he wish he were there now! And he wished that he had filled his pockets with some of those good things, but this was one adventure he hadn't planned to take.

At times, the water reached above his knees and made the wading slow. The muddy bottom sucked on his sneakers and made the journey all the more difficult. He paused a while on another gravel bar, wishing he didn't have to wade back into the cold water, but he knew there was no other way. Rescue would not come to him. He must be strong and courageous like a hunter on safari, wading through the worst crocodile infested swamps in Africa. He shuddered at the picture in his mind. Well, maybe not the worst swamp, he reconsidered, maybe just a short stretch of river across to Tarzan's tree house. Someplace crocodiles didn't like to hang out.

Slowly he waded back in up to his knees and pushed onward. Somewhere there had to be an opening, a ray of light. And Dugan the Daring would find it.

Suddenly something bumped into his leg again. Something large and soft that curled like a cat around his knee. Then it crawled up his right arm!

"Rat!" he shouted.

He leaped wildly backward, his arms flailing around like branches in a storm. He teetered and stumbled and struggled to keep his balance on the squishy floor. Was it following him? The tunnel went black. Suddenly he realized that in his panic he had dropped his flashlight into the water. He thought he heard native drums, and then realized it was his own heart. The bump on his head began to throb again. He shivered from his soggy sneakers to the tips of his hair, which felt to be straight up.

He wished with all his heart that he were home safe in his room. Without the light, he could not see in which direction the rat had gone or if it had gone at all. All he could see was a glow where the flashlight lay in the muddy bottom beneath the water. Darkness surrounded him, dank and spooky. He cringed at the thought of wading forward and reaching down into the cold water where he would be faced at eye level with anything that might be lurking there. He choked back a sob. The light lay between him and the way out and he had to have it. He took his first step forward.

"I've killed a million dragons, Mr. Rat," he said softly, "and dragons are way bigger than rats. Even big rats."

He continued to reassure himself as he moved toward the precious glow beneath the murk. He held his piece of sword tensely before him.

"Dragons are way bigger," he repeated.

Then his leg brushed the soft body again. He jumped and thrashed it wildly with his sword stub. In the dark he could not see it. He could not hear it. He could hear nothing except his own excited breathing and his thrashing upon the water. He dared not stop his flailing for he had no way to tell if he was out of danger.

At last, he was too tired to swing anymore. He stopped and stood there panting and listening. His flashlight was only a short ways away. He dived for it and fished it out of the mud. Then he quickly shined it around until it lit upon the creature.

A smile crept across his face, and then a giggle shook his stomach. A moment later he broke into delighted laughter. It was not a rat at all, nor anything of a living, harmful nature. It was only his felt hat, now flattened from his beating. The scarlet feather that had crawled up his arm drooped soggily.

He had forgotten his hat since his fall from outside and now grabbed it like a welcome friend. He tucked it under his arm and resumed his walk, not quite so frightened anymore. He was certain that at any minute he would see a circle of light in the ceiling and would soon be home.

The minutes passed and he walked and walked, but the light did not come. He grew more and more tired from wading in the mud and water. He paused and watched an old newspaper float by. The loneliness deepened. His spirits sagged a little more. He had already gone farther than he thought would be necessary. Why couldn't he find the way out? He choked back a sob and shined the light as far as it would reach. Then there at the end of the beam, the tunnel seemed to change. It appeared to grow larger. A cheer bubbled up from his toes and waited on his lips for the happy moment. He hurried toward it.

As he drew near, he could hear the sound of falling water. His confusion grew. It should have been getting lighter, but it wasn't. It was as dark as ever.

At last he stood at the entrance to a large

underground room. He shined his light from the floor to the ceiling and over every wall. It was like a cave in the center of a gigantic chunk of Swiss cheese. There were holes everywhere. Big holes. Small holes. Holes up high. Holes down low. From the holes poured water in great streams and small trickles. The water fell into a lake that covered the floor.

Dugan looked from hole to hole. There was not a clue to tell him which one of them he might have floated through. He could not possibly search them all. He could not even reach them all. Nor could he guess the depth of the murky water on the floor. The only part of the room that was not covered with water was a narrow ledge to his left.

Dugan was a fair swimmer, for at least a short ways, but he was too tired to think about anything like that. He couldn't even guess which hole to investigate first.

He inched his way a few feet along the ledge

to a large rock that jutted from the wall. Then he climbed upon it to rest. Tears as big as dragon scales rolled down his small cheeks. He sobbed loudly.

"Please, God, let me go home. I'll never leave my own yard again," he cried.

At last he was too tired to even cry. He turned off his light to save the batteries and fell asleep in a huddle against the damp wall.

Chapter Three

Figgins

He awakened to the same darkness, the same dampness, and the same loneliness. There was no way to tell what time it was or how long he had been gone. No way to know if it was night or day. He flicked his light back on and studied the holes around the room one by one.

"Eeny, meeny, miny, moe, which way would a dragon go?" he asked in desperation.

He had no more time to think before he heard a roaring whoosh like the flushing of a giant toilet. Suddenly the trickle from some of the tunnels burst into rushing cascades. The room began to fill more quickly than the downstream tunnels could carry the foaming water away. Dugan leaped to his feet and stared in fright. The water rose rapidly. The rock he stood upon began to disappear into the lake.

He looked for someplace to go. The only choice he had was a hole behind him about twice his size and just about chest high. He found a pebble beside him and tossed it through, then listened to hear how deep it was on the other side. Luck was momentarily with him. He heard it land just a short ways down. The rising water began rushing up his legs. There was no more time to hesitate. He reached through the hole and gripped the other side, then began to wriggle himself up and through. The water rose faster and faster. Too fast! His chest pounded. There isn't enough time to save myself, he thought. Even if he made it to whatever lay on the other side, the water would soon follow.

Suddenly he toppled through and landed on his hat, which had fallen through first. He grabbed it and his light and sprang to his feet. Now was his second bit of luck. The floor was a solid gravel bed with only a shallow stream of water covering it. The tunnel stretched into the distance as far as he could see and beyond.

Dugan began to run with his heart aflutter like hummingbird wings. There was no time to wonder where he was headed or if the tunnel was taking him deeper into the earth and farther away from home. The water, too, had reached the opening and chased down the corridor after him. It reached the top of his sneakers. It reached his knees. It pushed and gushed and threatened to knock him down, but he plodded on. He panted harder and harder and grew more and more tired and fearful. Then just when he thought he could run no more and that the water would wash him away, the flood began to ease. The water stopped rising, then began to quickly drop.

Dugan's whole body throbbed. He was so tired, he just wanted to lie down and sleep for a hundred hours. He shined his light and hoped for a small ledge or anyplace that was dry.

Suddenly his light reflected back off of two large white circles a few yards away. It was rather eerie, but he ventured a bit closer. The circles blinked. He jumped back and felt for his sword, but it was gone. His hands began to tremble. He glanced back the way he had come. He wanted desperately to turn and run, but he remembered there was no place to run back to.

"I'm D-D-Dugan the D-D-Daring," he stammered. "I can go anyplace a dragon can go, but please, don't be a dragon."

"Cru-bug, that's an eye popper," said a deep voice.

"What?" Dugan said, not at all believing his ears.

"Unlight me," the voice said.

Dugan lowered his flashlight.

"Who are you?" he asked.

"Infroggable you should ask. I've been here since I was a polydoodler," said the stranger.

"Well, I've only been here since I fell through a hole, and you look like a giant talking frog," said Dugan.

"Wart-be-gone, if you didn't guess it," said the frog.

Dugan moved closer. He had never seen such an enormous frog. It was almost as tall as he was. It had the look of a Persian rug or a magic carpet with the luminous intertwining of Lincoln green and indigo blue, marbled with copper and chartreuse and streaked with threads of silver. Dugan would have marveled longer at the frog's most amazing appearance had he not been so stunned by its voice.

"Frogs don't talk," Dugan said.

"Little boys don't play underground," said the frog.

"I'm not playing. I'm lost."

"Wart-be-gone, you're the first boy I ever saw, and you're even funnier looking than I imagined."

"I'm not funny looking," Dugan said. "This is the way boys are supposed to look."

"Scribbit, but you're touchy."

Dugan's light hit upon the chunk of a hot dog as it floated by. Quicker than Dugan could squeeze mustard on a new shirt, three feet of florescent orange tongue ribboned out of the frog's mouth. It did a loop-d-loop, a half back flip, a vertical wave, bounced off the water, then curled into a lariat and lassoed the hot dog. Then the one-tongue circus act slithered back in through the tight bronze lips and the frog sucked the hot dog down with a loud glup.

"Cru-bug," said the frog, his florescence suddenly ultra bright. "I ate the whole thing. I'm so embarrassed. My first alien visitor and I forget my dinner manners. I'll make it up to you. I'll catch you the first grub that floats by and a beetle to go with it."

Dugan's stomach did a roll. He was just about hungry enough to accept and that worried him.

"My mother doesn't allow me to eat with friends unless I ask her first. It'd spoil my dinner at home. She'll be mad enough already," he said to discourage any future offers.

From farther down the shaft came a gentle rhythmic slush of water. The frog forgot Dugan and shot his tongue three feet straight into the air, whirled it around like an orange tornado, then sucked it back into his face. He then stood on his front legs and thumped the back ones on the water before ending with a back flip.

"Why did you do that?" Dugan asked.

"I'm at that age, you know," said the frog.

"What age?"

'When I'm attracted by the opposite sex."

'What?"

"I am referring to the she-frog that is coming this way."

"You mean you have a girlfriend?"

"An infroggable beauty. Have you ever been in love?"

"I sort of liked the girl next door once," said Dugan. "I took my sword over to show her I was a knight, but she stuck her tongue out at me and said she was waiting for a prince. So I made her kiss a . . . a . . . my dog."

A second frog now appeared within Dugan's light. Except for being slightly smaller and having bright coral lips, Dugan could see little difference between the two.

"Well, stew me a fly," she snipped. "Look what the rain washed down."

"This is Stabella," said the frog in a half swoon.

"It's infroggable what you will play with, Figgins," said Stabella.

"He's okay. He's just a little boy."

"Just a little boy! Well, keep him away from me. I don't want him to give me warts."

"Little boys don't give you warts," Figgins said. "My cousin from the Great Out-There said . . ."

"I don't want to hear about your old cousin from the Out-There. I'm hungry," said Stabella.

Figgin's long tongue jitterbugged out, did a quick boogaloo, and a double wave before he snatched a fat ugly bug off the wall and offered it to Stabella.

"Stick it in your fly box. I can get my own," she said.

Figgins tongue instantly wilted onto the water and his big eyes rolled down sadly.

"I thought that was real super," Dugan said.

Figgins slowly offered his catch to Dugan, who did not even want to handle the hairy squirming lump.

"Thanks," he said, "but I'm allergic to gray hair on my lunch."

Figgins unhappily dragged his tongue back

into his mouth and gulped his catch. Then he
heaved a sigh of disappointment.

"Wanna hop?" he asked Stabella.

"I think I will," she said. 'Scribbit."

She smugly turned and hopped away,
swamping Dugan and Figgins with the wake
she left behind.

"She's not very nice," Dugan said.

"She's beautiful," said Figgins. "She makes
my eyes bug."

"My mother says a girl is only as beautiful
as she acts."

"She's just puffed today," Figgins said in her
defense. "I wish my cousin was here from the Great
Out-There. He's an infroggable whiz at love."

"Is that where I live? The Great Out-There?"

"Well, stew me a fly, don't you know where
you live?"

"I know where I live. I just don't know
where I am."

"You should have asked Stabella" Figgins

said. "I'm not one to venture. I'm your local hopper. But Stabella is a dare-terror. She hops inter-tunnel. She'd hop right on out into the Out-There, except she thinks that's where inferior life glogs live. You noticed how she didn't social interlate with you. That might be her one shortcoming. She never sees the beauty in oddity. I think it's her family. They live on a large pond."

"Sometimes people who live on big ponds aren't very friendly either. They put keep-out signs in their yards," Dugan said. "Maybe there's something in the water like crab-pox."

Figgins sighed. "I'd catch anything to catch Stabella."

Dugan looked down the tunnel in the direction Stabella had gone. The waves had settled and all trace of her had vanished. Dugan was ever so weary, but he couldn't rest now. He had to find her. She might be his only chance to find his way out.

"It was nice talking to you," Dugan said, "but I better hurry and catch her. Maybe some day when I get home I'll meet your cousin."

Figgins bright orange tongue flithered out and slid across the water to snare a soggy morsel.

He gulped, then sighed, "Must I always dine alone?"

Dugan waved as he hastened on down the tunnel hoping he could find Stabella and that she would find just enough niceness in her prickly little heart to help him.

Chapter Four

Giant Peeper

Until he met Figgins, Dugan had seen no bugs or creatures at all. But as he trudged along in his search for Stabella, he spied more of the gray hairy bugs Figgins had offered him for lunch. He also now saw other strange insects and spider-like creatures that walked upon the water. The strangest of all the critters he saw were little worms that poked their heads out of the wall, each from its own little hole. Their white heads were banded in black around their eyes, which made them appear as though they wore masks. They watched him very boldly and very intently in their curiosity, like peepers. A most unworm-like habit.

Dugan's interest in them was only brief. He was incredibly hungry and thirsty. He had not had a thing to eat or drink since before he turned the sprinklers on Mrs. Murphy's table. That seemed a hundred years ago. He wished he could tell her he was sorry.

He stopped and took a close look at the shallow water he waded in. It looked clean enough here, but his mom had told him never to drink water from anywhere except a clean faucet unless an adult told him it was safe. But there was no faucet here or adult to direct him and not even a doctor's tongue depressor was as dry as his own tongue was now. Perhaps, he thought, this one time will be all right. He scooped up a handful of water, and then watched a moldy clump of green goopy slime float by. His stomach twinged. He let the water trickle out of his fingers. What was he to do?

He leaned against the wall and let his flashlight hang down at the end of his arm. He dropped his chin onto his chest. If only someone was here to tell me what to do, he thought. This was the biggest problem he had ever faced, a Morgan Peckles-size problem. How he wished his dad were there to invent a way home.

Then he realized how much warmer the water had become, even pleasantly so. The tunnel had also grown lighter. He shut off his light, and then cheered. He could see perfectly well without it. It could mean only one thing - he had reached a way out! Somewhere nearby there had to be an opening that the sun was shining through. It was surely large enough for a small boy to escape through.

He began to run. He ran and ran. He ran past other tunnels that branched off on both sides. He ran past dozens of ugly bugs and masked peepers.

The tunnel grew lighter and lighter. He panted and looked. Looked and panted. Half exuberated. Half frantic. He looked and looked. Still the tunnel stretched on and on with no sign of a break to the outside world.

At last, too tired and out of breath to go on anymore, he dropped onto a large boulder jutting from the wall. He drooped his tired head and rested his chin in his hands. He could not understand it. He had come a long ways. He should have found something by now. The water was warm. The tunnel was light. Where was the sun shining through?

As he thought, he looked at the rock he sat upon. It had a faint glow and was as warm as if the summer sun had shone upon it all day. He looked up and searched above his head. Then he noticed the walls were lined with white stone and that the white stones glowed. The light and warmth did not come from the sun. It came from the rocks. There was no way out here and he had lost Stabella.

He leaned back and stared at the wall across from him. A small stream of water trickled down over the layers of stone. It looked clean and clear. The pale rocks made it sparkle. Right or wrong, he had no choice. He was too thirsty to wait any longer. He filled his hands and drank a long time.

When he finished, he sat upon the rock and leaned against the wall again for a few moments rest. That's when he noticed a work crew of large transparent green ants. Their heads were capped with tiny rounded shells that looked like hardhats worn by workmen. They were busy chewing the pale green stalks of plants that resembled queer little spaceships with juicy purple globes on the top. He named them purple-pops. Each time the cutter ants toppled a purple-pop, another crew dragged it to a row of holes in the wall. There, other workers like long-legged tankers sucked the juice from the globes, then disappeared into the holes. The next team chewed the stalks into small pieces, which they stuffed into pouches on the fronts of their bodies. Then they, too, bustled into the holes to store their goods in their nest.

Dugan could have sat and watched them for hours if he hadn't been so hungry himself. He had been taught never to pick and eat unfamiliar plants. Some were full of vitamins and good to eat, but some were poisonous and could mean death even in small amounts. Now his stomach was so empty, if he didn't eat, he wouldn't have the strength to go on, and he wouldn't survive to make it home.

He hesitated only a moment longer, and then he plucked a large shimmering purple-pop. It had the mild pleasant scent of a fruity blend. He studied it a moment longer, not knowing what he was looking for. He glanced at the ants again to see if any of them would fall over dead. They continued their business with speed and gusto. Dugan knew that just because it was okay for ants still didn't mean it was okay for boys. There seemed to be no choice. He had to eat.

Dugan opened his mouth and stuck the large purple globe against his lips. He ran his tongue against it, and then gave a mighty slurp. The globe burst and gushed into his mouth. It had the cool freshness of a cucumber, the slight tang of lemon, and just a hint of watermelon and cherries. And it felt like carbonated gelatin as it slid down softly. Then he ate the stalk and couldn't quite decide if it tasted more like mint or bubblegum. It was a mouthful of mystery. It was something a wizard would have dreamed up while walking in the forest. It was tongue toy. A smile popped onto his face at the sheer pleasure of the funnest food he'd ever found.

He waited a moment after it slid down, a little frightened, a little curious. When nothing terrible happened, he began to pick and pop them into his mouth as quickly as he could. They were slurpy. They were tingly. They even made him giggle. And best of all, they had the curious affect of energy balls. Now he didn't feel so tired. In fact, he didn't feel tired at all. He renamed them magic-pep-pops.

When he'd eaten his fill, he picked some more. He squeezed the globes into his small empty canteen that hung on his belt and promised himself that forever after he would always keep it filled with clean water. He stuffed the stalks into empty jacket pockets.

His chores done, the time had come for another decision. He stood in the center of the tunnel and looked in both directions. Neither way showed any more promise. At last, he decided he would go back the way he had come, if he could find it, and search for Stabella.

As he walked along, he noticed a great many more of the odd little worms with their black masks. They peeped like bandits from their holes. Their eyes were boldly white against their black masks and followed Dugan as he passed by. He shivered. They gave him the creeps. When he glanced back, he was startled to see them stretched half way out of their holes, their milky white jelly-like bodies bent in his direction. They continued to spy on him with haunting eyes for as far as they could see. Creepier shivers ran through him. The peepers were almost ghostly with the light of the rocks glowing dully through their bodies. A wide band encircled their mid-section, like the night crawlers he and his dad had found on the street after a hard rain.

As Dugan walked, he now noticed that all the hairy gray bugs and other insects had disappeared. He began to smell a foul, awful odor that he had not noticed before. It smelled much like the can of night crawlers that had died and rotted in his closet, but a zillion times worse.

Within a few steps the smell had become so terrible he could hardly breathe. His eyes watered. He could even taste the wretched smell. He scanned the tunnel for the source of the odor. Then he glanced up. Terror struck him like a witch's curse. His heart punched his ribs. His breathing stopped. From the ledge above him, a giant peeper rolled off and landed at his feet. It encircled Dugan as quickly as if he'd fallen into a bowl of gelatin, and the way the peeper's slippery skin and milky insides wobbled, Dugan felt for a moment like that's just what he did.

Dugan squirmed and stretched his neck to keep his head out of his captor's coils. He struggled to kick his legs and flap his arms in an attempt to free himself. The peeper held tight, unmoved by Dugan's struggles. It raised its coils to capture Dugan's face, but Dugan wiggled and stretched and fought its efforts. Ripples of irritation fluttered through the peeper's gelatinous body. Then suddenly it rolled over in the shallow water that covered the tunnel floor. Dugan caught his breath just before his head went under. He came up with a gasp, then gasped again when he found himself face to black masked face with the hideous creature.

The peeper readjusted its coils in another effort to capture Dugan's head. Dugan quickly dodged and poked his head out between the coils. The peeper shifted again. Again Dugan's head popped out eye to eye. Back and forth they went. In and out of coils. Tossing. Grasping. Rolling. Gasping. Each was strongly determined. But Dugan soon began to weary. The peeper was slippery and fast. It was also well rested and six times Dugan's size. It could feel Dugan move slower and slower as his strength began to fade. Time was on the peeper's side. Dugan was near to exhaustion.

Next, the peeper began to ripple against Dugan like waves upon the sea. Dugan thought he was going to be seasick.

At last, Dugan lay still, unable to struggle anymore. His arms were pressed against him. His strength and hope were all but gone. Then for the first time, he realized his hands rested upon his utility belt. Beneath his right hand hung his pouch of rock salt. Dugan knew that salt melted ice, stung cuts, and cured sore throats. He knew cows and deer liked to lick it. He had heard you could catch a bird by sprinkling salt on its tail. Nowhere in his memory was there any mention of salt and worms.

Slowly he worked the clasp open and withdrew a handful of crystals. At first the peeper took Dugan's stillness for defeat. It continued to roll against him, sure that lunch was about to be had. Then Dugan opened his hand and rubbed the salt against the filmy skin. The peeper pulled away in annoyance. Dugan dropped the crystals into the coils and felt the creature wriggle in further discomfort. He pulled another pinch from his pouch and then another. Each time, the salt stung and dried the tender skin and caused the peeper to thrash wilder. Its coils loosened.

Dugan's stomach rolled with the roll of the worm, and his face grew greener by the second. He was about to regret his daring when a wild lunge by the creature hung the band around its middle upon a hook on Dugan's belt. Suddenly something very warm and oozy began to run down Dugan's leg. The band unzipped with a whoosh. The coils began to shrink and flatten. The black mask rumpled up before Dugan's face and collapsed over the big white eyes that stared in wide surprise. From the hole it had torn in itself, its milky insides flowed out until only a limp bag lay at Dugan's feet.

Chapter Five

The Gnōmystic

Dugan hastily looked around him. All the other little peepers had disappeared into their holes. He was glad. He didn't want to see another one of any size. He wanted to run and get away. He needed to find Stabella and quick! As he was about to head back, he realized his hat was gone. It must have fallen off during the struggle and floated down stream. He paused a moment, then decided it should only take a minute or two to chase it down, so he turned back again.

He had not gone far before he came to a fork in the tunnel that he had passed earlier. The hat could have gone either way, but the second tunnel ran a bit more downhill and the water ran slightly faster. On a quick guess, he chose the new course. He further reasoned that since he had not found Stabella on the first path, perhaps she had taken this tunnel as well.

It proved to be a lucky choice, for he had not gone far before he spied the runaway hat several yards ahead. He chased after it, but before he could catch it, a new stream of water shot up from the floor and changed the slow moving stream to a rushing creek. The slight decline gave way to a winding, dipping water raceway. Dugan ran faster, but no matter how fast he ran, the hat moved faster. Whenever he gained a little ground, the hat dipped or whirled or sped ahead. Dugan knew he was going farther and farther away from where he wanted to go, but he just couldn't give up when his favorite hat was so close to his grasp.

Then the hat swirled around a small eddy and bumped against the wall where it came to a brief halt. Dugan took a deep sigh of relief and reached for it. As he bent forward he realized his careless error. The hat broke free and took a dip. Dugan lunged and fell headlong down the longest water slide he had ever seen. He sailed wildly, picking up speed. Picking up speed. Zig. Zag. Zig. Zag. Round piles of rock. Picking up speed. Through narrow passages. Picking up speed. The course humped and bumped and twisted around. Water jets from the walls shot out and rolled him front to back and end to end. He slid every way except standing on his head, and then found himself sitting upright.

Suddenly the channel took a sharp right turn. His eyes popped and his jaw dropped. Right before his face a solid wall appeared, moments away from collision and no way to stop. Then just as his nose was about to part the moss on the stone, the slide suddenly dropped sharply, throwing him onto his back at the last moment. He felt feathery branches tickle his face as he slid under the wall and raced down a chute barely larger than himself. Then the small tube broadened and he zoomed down the last stretch and shot out into a great cavern. At the bottom of the slide, he came to rest near a pool.

The sudden relief from sheer fright drained every ounce of strength from him. He lay upon the ground limp as a plastic bag full of pudding. His hat lay beside him. Wearily he tucked it under his arm as his only comfort. There was no time for thoughts of further danger or to wonder about where he had come to rest. His head rolled onto a large tuft of puffy burgundy leaves and his eyes closed in utter exhaustion.

Dugan awoke to a thump, thump, thump upon his head. At first he thought he was home and under playful attack by his Scotch terrier.

"Dargon. Dargon," he muttered.

Slowly he opened his eyes. Beside him stood

an odd little man with a long wooden shaft, which he used to thump Dugan upon the head. Dugan sat up with a frown and rubbed the spot.

"Why are you hitting me?" he asked.

"Why indeed!" came the answer.

The attacker was very short and exceedingly thin with bare bony arms and legs. His knees and feet were gnarled like old tree roots and his toes were extra long. There was a sixth toe protruding on the outside of each foot. These toes tapped upon the ground as though they were feeling their way along. The man's complexion was a cross between a russet potato and an old carrot. He would have looked dirty even if he bathed twice a day, but looked as though he seldom bathed at all.

"Are you a midget?" Dugan asked, thinking a troll would be closer to the truth.

"As if you didn't know I am the great Gnomystic, Prompong Peerapool," came the sharp reply.

Prompong raised his shaft to rap Dugan again, but Dugan sprang to his feet and raised his arms for protection in the karate pose his dad had taught him.

"Don't hit me again," he said. "I don't like it."

The gnomystic paused. He no longer had the advantage. Dugan was nearly as tall as he was, sturdier looking, and prepared to defend himself. They stared at each other.

The top of the little man's head was very round and very bald. Not even a whisper of eyebrows traced his high forehead. A bushy blue-black beard grandly hid the lower part of his face. Between the desert of his crown and the forest of his chin sat an enormous nose that from the side looked like a bird wing in flight. Ears, like giant kidney beans, were half the length of his head.

But what Dugan found the most curious and the most disturbing were Prompong's large pea-green eyes. While one eye carefully studied

Dugan, the other eye wandered lazily around the cavern as though it belonged to someone else and had nothing to do. Dugan often found his own gaze trying to follow that of the roving eye. Then he decided it was a trick to distract him, and determined not to let it. He fought hard to keep his gaze upon the suspicious little man.

"You think you're very clever, don't you?" said Prompong. "But your incantation won't work here. You can't read my pool."

"Incantation?" Dugan said. "Do you mean like a magic spell?"

Prompong beat his shaft upon the ground while he stamped his feet.

"I heard you. I heard you," he said. "But Dargon is not on the list from the Great Paramoos. You can't use it here."

"Dargon is my dog," Dugan said. "He usually follows me, but sometimes he's with Mom and doesn't see me go out."

Prompong quickly searched around him.

"I see nothing with you," he said, "except that thing you hold."

Dugan took his hat from under his arm and fluffed it up the best he could after the beating it had taken since his fall. He fluffed up the big crimson plume. As he held it before him in momentary admiration, Prompong made a hasty grab, but Dugan withdrew it faster and plopped it upon his head. It made his own size appear greater.

"I always wear it for luck," he said. "I'm Dugan the Daring."

The gnomystic brought both eyes together with a snap and stared at Dugan more suspiciously. He feared this new gnome-type creature with the peculiar but enviable head topper might be even more powerful than he appeared. Prompong silently coveted the unusual coverings the new-one wore, but sneered to himself on the misfortune of the odd-one's misplaced hair upon the top of his head instead of upon his chin.

"What means three rings upon the Pool?" he asked.

"Is that like skipping a rock three times, because I can do that," Dugan said.

The answer did not please the gnomystic. He was not familiar with skipping a rock three times. Perhaps that was more powerful than three rings. He squinted a bit. The one eye studied Dugan more closely. The other alternated glancing from one side of the cavern to the other and up and down Dugan, not at all convinced Dugan was alone.

"What are the seven depths?" Prompong asked.

"I'm hungry," Dugan said, ignoring another question that made no sense. "Don't you have some peanut butter, hamburgers, French fries, pickles, watermelon, barbecue, pumpkin pie?"

Looking at the gnomystic, Dugan knew there wasn't a chance the answer would be a happy one. The irritable little man was so skinny he could almost hide behind his own shaft. Dugan knew from comments by neighbor ladies to his mom that half of them would give a pirate's treasure to know the secret of his skinniness. Dugan would rather have peanut butter and chocolate milk.

"If you could do aerobics, women would love you on TV," Dugan said, trying to be friendly.

"What is TV?" Prompong asked, his curiosity slightly greater than his fear of looking the fool.

"A picture in a box. You can watch things at home that are far away. My dad's an inventor and he says it's quite amazing that waves in the air can make little dots that we see as pictures. But Mom just smiles when he says things like that. She says in a world looked after by angels anything is possible. So I ask my angels to make me an inventor like Dad. But if I don't grow up to be an inventor like him, I might be a magician. Mom would probably like me to be a saint, but I think that's kind of a magician too.

Except saints don't get into as much trouble as I do. Right now I could use a little less trouble."

Both of Prompong's eyes focused on Dugan. For an instant, Dugan thought he saw them bulge. Prompong's ears vibrated with frustration. The orange tinge of his face turned pasty.

"What does a gnomystic do?" Dugan asked.

The little man puffed out his skinny chest in indignation. He drew himself up inside the white wrappings that served him for clothing and gave him the appearance of playing peek-a-boo in a pile of dirty bed sheets.

"I told you. I am Prongpong Peerapool. I read the mystic waters."

"I wish you could read my mind and stomach, because they're yelling I'm hungry."

"Where do you come from? How did you get here?" Prompong asked, ignoring the conversation Dugan most wanted.

"I guess I'm from the Great Out-There. I fell through a hole."

There was a slight gasp, and then a long hmmmmmm as Prompong continued to study him and speculate on Dugan's power and position.

"Do you know about the Out-There?" Dugan said.

"Prompong Peerapool reads the mystic waters and knows all things," he said.

"Then why don't you know who I am? Why do you ask me all these questions?"

Prompong hesitated. His roving eye dropped down and stared at his bare feet. His outside toes tapped about uncertainly.

"I was testing you," he said at last.

"If you were lost and came to my house, my mom would give you milk and cookies and sandwiches," Dugan hinted. "She would probably slice you an apple and put peanuts by your napkin."

Dugan's words didn't seem to reach Prompong. The gnomystic rubbed his head three times in one direction, then twice in the other. He tipped his head from side to side and pondered.

"I have grown a hunger in this confusion," he said. "It is time to fire the rashoo."

Prompong turned and walked away as though Dugan had disappeared. Dugan hesitated and then trailed after him. He still had no idea of what was about to be served, but he was hungry enough to take a chance if he could get an invitation to dinner.

As they approached a pile of thin brittle twigs, Prompong suddenly halted, placed one hand over his eyes, and pointed toward the pool with his shaft.

"Ah, it comes to me now," he said. "It was only a dream span ago that I stood beside the pool. A circle appeared upon the surface. Yes, red, just the color of the fern upon your headpiece. It floated through the first depth, skittered in confusion, just as you have done. It behaved most strangely. I thought it quite queer. But just at that time, I had to turn the peeper skins upon the drying rail. If I had but stayed longer, I would have seen all that has passed between us."

"Sounds like you need a pool recorder," Dugan said.

Prompong paused briefly, but did not want to admit again that the stranger knew something he did not. So he bent to his task of rubbing two shiny rocks together, one white, one green. Soon a spark leaped into the pile of twigs and they burst into flames. Shortly after, they settled into an even red glow.

"What are peeper skins?" Dugan asked.

Prompong looked at him with surprise.

"You do not know the peepers?" he said. "You smell very much like a peeper."

Dugan held his jacket to his nose. It still carried the odor of the huge white worm.

"Of course, you could not know the peepers, at least not a peeper of skinning size or you would not be here to ask. Only a gnomystic with the powers and skills of the first ranked could live to tell of an encounter with a giant peeper," Prompong boasted.

He proudly rubbed the white wrappings he wore.

"Is a peeper a big white worm? It has a mask like a bandit. Zorro has a mask like that, but he doesn't jump on the good guys."

Prompong was near exasperation, "A peeper is not a worm! It is a peeper! It is white and grows to great size if its life days are long and undisturbed. It wears a black mask to hide its wicked face."

"One almost got me!" Dugan said excitedly, "but I fought and I fought until it shriveled up and melted."

Prompong plunked down beside the fire in an annoyed pout. His skinny body drooped. One eye watched the fire, while the other wandered back and forth from Dugan and the farthest point of the cavern. Dugan dropped upon a large stone beside the fire. His clothes had not entirely dried and the warmth and drying power of the fire felt especially welcome.

"Fighting peepers makes me hungry," Dugan said.

Prompong reached into a lidded basket and pulled out three large bronze colored beetles. He tossed them upon the glowing coals. They sizzled until they popped open like popcorn. Inside was a mouthful of tender white meat. With a pair of tongs he had fashioned from metal strips that had worked their way down from the outside world, he placed the hot rashoo on a flat rock beside him. He tossed another handful into the fire, and then popped the meat of a cooked one into his mouth.

Dugan waited a few moments for his host to invite him to eat, then helped himself when it became obvious that he would be left to starve if he waited for Prompong to invite him. With the hair burned off and the shell cracked, the white meat even looked rather appealing. But at this point, Dugan was less than picky. He slipped the meat into his mouth and found it quite tasty.

"This is good," he said. "Maybe sometime when we go camping I could show my mom how to cook some. My mom never cooked bugs before."

"She does not fire the rashoo?" Prompong asked in amazement. "Then what fills the hole of your hunger?"

"Do you mean what do we eat?" Dugan said. "Chicken or steak or mashed potatoes or apple pie."

"It does not sound very good," Prompong said.

Prompong reached behind him with his tongs and twisted a clump of mossy growth off the cavern wall. He warmed it on the fire, and then dropped it on the stone between him and Dugan. Dugan pulled a few strands for himself. It was stringy and coarse, but rather fun like shoestring potatoes or spaghetti. Prompong sat silently staring into the fire.

"Is it hard being a gnomystic?" Dugan asked. "It's hard being a kid these days. Trying to think if you should be a knight or a space walker. Of course, there aren't any knights anymore, but it's expensive to be a space walker."

Prompong's one roving eye sneaked a side-glance at Dugan, who was thinking a gnomystic was one thing he did not want to be. When he had eaten his fill of rashoo, he thanked his host.

Chapter Six

Working his Way Home

Now that he was no longer hungry, Dugan's natural curiosity came back and he began to think about his strange companion.

"Why do you read a pool?" he asked.

"It tells the future and the past, I have been chosen for this task," Prompong said.

"Who chose you?"

Prompong hesitated. His trick eye rolled around twice, then dropped to the floor.

"Destiny chose me to read for all creaturekind."

"Can you tell me how to get home?"

Prompong's hands fidgeted. His whiskers twitched.

"Why . . . why, of course, I can."

"Could you tell me now," Dugan asked excitedly. "My mom gets scared when she doesn't know where I am. She'll think someone stole me, and she'll cry. I hate it when my mom cries. It makes me sad. Can I go home now?"

Prompong jumped up, grabbed his shaft and began to hurry away.

"I can't tell you just like that," he said.

"If you know, why not?" Dugan said and trailed after him. "I'd tell you if you were lost."

"Gnomystics are different. They cannot just tell. You have not done anything to earn it. The pool does not read for those who do not work."

"I work," Dugan said. "I help my mother all the time. I can dust and water flowers and wash dishes. I help my dad wash the car and work on his inventions."

Prompong stopped and turned indignantly toward him.

"The pool does not care what you do for your mother, but a great gnomystic like myself does not need help from anyone."

"Please let me help," Dugan begged. "I'm a good helper. The pool will like me if you let me help."

"I guess I have no choice," Prompong said. "It is my destiny and duty to serve. The Pool has spoken. Follow me."

As they walked along the edge of the large pool that Prompong spoke about, the gnomystic walked cautiously, far from the edge. Dugan liked water, except for his recent sogginess, and walked very close to it. He had never seen water so clear. The bottom was covered with beautiful jewel-like pebbles in all the colors he had ever seen and some he hadn't. They sparkled with a brilliance that seemed to dance through the water. It looked to be no deeper than he could stand in.

He had an empty pocket he could fill and thought how grand it would be to take some of the beautiful stones home to his mother. He had promised her that someday he would buy her a diamond necklace as big as a queen would wear, because she was the greatest mom in any kingdom. Maybe she would like the pretty stones just as much. He paused and knelt beside the water to take a closer look. Prompong's stern voice stopped him from dipping his hand.

"Do not touch the Pool," he shouted. "Take care not to fall in!"

Dugan looked puzzled.

"It's not very deep," Dugan said. "I could stand up in it."

"That is one of its tricks. It is so clear, it fools you. It is very deep."

"Oh. Well, I can swim."

"You will not swim in this pool."

Then Dugan began to notice that there were very strange and scary creatures swimming about.

"Those are weird fish," he said.

"A mystery you cannot guess," said Prompong.

Dugan walked slowly around the edge of the pool, his attention focused on the strange inhabitants while Prompong hurried on his way.

"Weird," Dugan repeated to himself. "When I go fishing with Dad, I hope we never catch one of these."

Near the top of the water, small ugly mustard-yellow fish darted about fearfully. They swam as though they swam for their lives even though nothing chased them. They only paused now and then but when they did, they trembled and watched guardedly.

As Dugan studied the pool further, he discovered there were several types of fish in the water but none of them mixed with the others. Each stayed in its own layer and away from all the rest.

Beneath the yellow darters swam dark creatures, knobby and crusted. They blackened the water around them so that each swam in its own fouled cloud.

In the third layer, the bellies of the fish hung like bags so stuffed, they looked ready to burst. The weight of them flopped from side to side with every movement. When the fish tried to stay still the belly weight pulled them heavily downward. Big bulging eyes darted back and forth, never resting. When Dugan tried to rapidly shift his eyes as the fish did, his stomach went queasy.

The layer that held the most occupants came next. The inhabitants here had great ugly mouths that gaped and never closed. Their tongues streamed out like whips with barbs and beat the sides of their owners.

As he looked deeper, Dugan took great care to keep his balance so he wouldn't fall in. He did not like the looks of these creatures.

In the fifth depth, the fish were so enormously puffed up, they appeared to be on the verge of exploding. Their scales were heavy and gaudy like old jewelry the little girl next door wore when she played dress-up. On the front of each was a very pig-like snout.

Near the bottom, the dwellers were even uglier. They were made up of parts from nature's most loathed creatures. They had the tail of a vulture, skin of a lizard, tongue of a snake, and ears of a rat. Their side fins mimicked bat wings. Dugan shuddered.

He now thought he had seen them all and started to hurry after Prompong, but then he paused again. At the very bottom, almost hidden among the colored stones, lived the most frightful of all. There were only a few at this last level. Dugan could not guess if they stayed so far apart because they liked to be alone or because of their horrid bodies. They were covered with barbs and thorns and blade-like fins, which would have torn each other apart if they came too close. Dugan marveled that a pond so beautiful could hold such horrid creatures.

He wanted to ask Prompong about them, but Prompong had reached the wall at the other side of the cavern and was waiting impatiently. Dugan hurried to catch up. The little man scowled and his one eye bounced up and down like a ping-pong ball.

"I'm sorry," Dugan said when he caught up. "It's just that the pool…"

"Yes, the Pool. You said what you wished to do was please the Pool, was it not?"

"Yes, but… "

"The Pool does not understand buts. It understands work."

"I'm ready," Dugan said.

On the wall behind Prompong, Dugan spied a curtain of tightly woven roots. Prompong pulled it back slightly to expose a cave hidden behind it. He motioned Dugan to enter. Dugan stepped forward to take a look.

"Yikes!" he shouted and jumped back, but Prompong blocked the way out.

There was scarcely an inch of the walls or ceiling that did not crawl with rust-hued rashoo. Prompong shoved a lidded basket into Dugan's hands and motioned for him to move deeper into the cave.

"You must gather the next meal," he said. "A basketful will do for a start. But it must be full!"

Dugan cringed. A big plump rashoo dropped from the ceiling, landed on his arm, and then sat there twitching its antennae. Dugan brushed it off.

"I'm not going to catch a whole basketful of bugs," he said. "It's creepy in here."

"The choice is yours," Prompong said. "I cannot make the Pool serve a loafer."

"You mean I won't go home?" Dugan's face dropped in dismay.

He glanced around the walls again. They were a solid mass of wriggling bugs. His skin crawled. He tried to take another step backward.

"Isn't there something else I could do?"

Prompong sighed loudly. "The tears of your mother flow through my mind."

Dugan gulped. He could not bear the thought of his mother crying and he had to get home, whatever it took. Reluctantly, he took the basket. Prompong shoved him forward.

"Toward the back they are a bit fatter," he said.

Dugan was usually not fussy about bugs, but then he was usually not surrounded on all sides by millions of them. He plucked one from the wall and dropped it into the basket. It promptly scurried out. He caught another and this time quickly slammed the lid after it. He caught another, but when he raised the lid to toss it in, the first one scrambled out. For the next few minutes, his efforts continued to fail while Prompong stood in the doorway snickering.

"It's not funny," Dugan said.

He set the basket down and folded his arms.

"Have it your way," Prompong said. "I must consult the Pool soon. An empty basket earns empty answers."

He stepped out, dropped the curtain and left Dugan alone. Tears rose behind Dugan's eyes. The ache in his heart grew. Would he ever get home? He slowly turned, observing the thousands of bugs. How could he get enough to stay in the basket so the pool would be happy and tell him the way home? It seemed so long ago that he had kissed his mom or played ball with his dad or crawled through the doggie door in the kitchen with Dargon.

"The doggie door!" he said.

He removed his penknife from his belt. It had one small blade that wasn't very sharp and his dad had taught him to use it safely. Even if he didn't remember to stay in his own yard, he always did remember the safe use of his tools.

He shoved the lid tightly on the basket and

made three short cuts in the top. He pushed on the small door he had made, and then smiled. He caught a bug and shoved it through, then another and another. It worked! He could push them in and guard the door so they could not get back out. He worked faster and faster. He became so excited he even forgot how creepy it was to be in a room full of bugs. He snatched them from the wall and shoved them in through the door. He began to hum a going-home song that he made up as he went along. He soon had the basket full. He smiled to himself. Only a short while ago he had thought it was impossible. He could hardly wait to tell his dad about his invention. He hurried to the woven curtain and pulled a corner up high enough to get out.

As he took a last look at the wriggling cave, he called out, "Dugan the Daring, the winner!"

The basketful of rashoo was rather heavy. He trudged around the pool, holding the basket tightly in front of him. He was careful not to get too close to the edge. Twice he had to stop to rest, but he didn't rest long. He was too anxious to learn what the pool had told Prompong while he worked.

When he finally arrived at the campsite, he found Prompong asleep on a woven mat. Dugan nudged him. Prompong grumbled and rolled over, ignoring him. Dugan nudged him again.

"I filled the basket," he said. "Did the pool tell you how I get home?"

"The Pool said I should sleep, and if you were worthy, the answer would come in my dreams."

"Did the answer come?" Dugan said. "I want to go home now. I filled the basket like you said. I want to go home now."

Prompong reluctantly sat up and took the heavy basket from him.

"My dreams were empty," he said. "How did you keep the rashoo in the basket?"

Dugan proudly showed him the beetle door he had cut in the lid.

Prompong walked to a nearby rock and tore off a sprig of blue-green plant.

"Myself, I crush a bit of the weary weed and drop it into the basket," he said. "It makes them fall asleep so they can't crawl out".

"Why didn't you tell me?" Dugan said, angrily. "They were crawling all over."

"Do you expect me to do everything for you? I am far too busy with more important things."

The gnomystic began to wander around, and his trick eye wandered even more. Dugan followed after him.

"You're not keeping your promise. When can I go home?" he demanded to know.

"It seems to me you have not yet earned the Pool's favor."

"Then tell me what to do," Dugan pleaded. "Please let me help you some more. I want to go home!"

"Oh, very well," Prompong said. "Why must I be of service to every creature that passes my way? It is a burden to be great and gifted."

Dugan hung his head.

"I'm sorry," he said. "I don't mean to be a bother, but I'm just a little kid and I'm lost. Don't you understand?"

Prompong led the way to a corner of the cavern where a clear stream tumbled from the wall and ran across the floor. Nearby sat two vats and a bucket constructed of wood-like material. Upon the wall climbed a lush mossy green plant dotted with brilliant pink flowers that smelled sweet and fragrant.

"This task is very simple," Prompong said. "You need only fill one vat with flowers you pick from the wall. But it must be full. Then with your bare feet you stomp upon the flowers until they are changed into sweet juice. Lastly, you fill the vat with water from the spring. When you are through, I can ask the Pool if it finds you worthy of assistance."

"That will take me hours," Dugan said sadly.

"The Pool knows no time," Prompong said. "I will return to my dreams so that I may dream the answer to your question."

He left Dugan alone again, but Dugan was now so tired, even picking the little flowers was a chore. He sat down beside the wall and slowly plucked the ones near the bottom and dropped them into the bucket. Within moments the picking stopped altogether, his head dropped and he slumped against the wall in weary sleep.

He awoke to a thump upon his head and found Prompong again tapping him with his shaft.

"Don't hit me with that," Dugan said. "I told you I don't like that."

Prompong stared into the bucket. The flowers scarcely covered the bottom.

"Is this the way you pay the Pool? A loafer. Truly you are! Unworthy of even the slightest ripple upon the mystical Pool."

"I'm not a loafer. I'm just very, very tired," Dugan said.

He began to pick the flowers again. The gnomystic stood by and scowled at him. Then after a few minutes, the odd little man wandered away mumbling about the unfairness of serving others.

It seemed a long time before Dugan had filled the first bucket of flowers. He dumped them into the vat, and then stared in at the vast emptiness. It was going to take a lot of buckets to fill it. A lot of buckets and a long time! His head drooped. He plodded back to the wall and began to pick again, slowly at first.

While he picked, he dreamed about home. He remembered the times he had played with Dargon and how glad his dog would be to have him home. He picked a little faster and then dumped his next bucket.

He thought about his dad and smiled about the fun they had and games they played. He thought about swimming at the lake and playing in the park. He picked a little faster and dumped the bucket again. He thought about how important he felt when he helped Dad with chores, when they raked the yard and dove in the leaves, when they washed the cars and sprayed each other. He thought about how good it felt when Dad told him he did a good job. He dumped another bucket and ran back to the wall. Dad would be glad to have him home. He would scold Dugan for leaving his yard, but he would still be glad.

He thought about his mother. He thought about stories she read to him. He thought about working in the garden together and picking red tomatoes and cutting flowers to set in the house. He dumped another bucket and picked a little faster. He thought about the good lunches Mom fixed him and the jokes she told while he ate. He laughed when he remembered his favorites. He dumped another bucket and another. When he got home she would scold him, too and would probably cry, but she would cry because she was glad.

He thought about his Guardian Angel who Mom said was always with him, and probably the busiest angel in heaven. He felt a smile spread across his heart, because with his angel, even when he made mistakes, things turned out okay. So he whispered to his angel to take care of him and help him get home. He whispered to her to tell his mom he was okay and would be home soon. Mom knew how angels talked. He thanked his angel for her help.

He dumped another bucket and another, and the next thing he knew the vat was full of beautiful brilliant pink flowers. The fragrance was the best smell he had ever smelled, like an angel tea party, he decided. He wished Mom were here. She loved flowers better than just about anything.

Dugan took off his sneakers and rolled up his jeans and climbed up the two steps on the outside to the top of the vat. For a moment he looked down into the lake of pink, then laughed as he jumped in. The flowers popped and squished like tiny water balloons filled with sweet slippery oil. They slid between his toes and tickled his feet. They colored him pink up to his knees. For a while he forgot his cares and stomped around laughing more and more. The pop, pop beneath his feet was more fun than popping plastic shipping wrap. I could sell this at a carnival, he thought.

"Get your tickets to the world's funniest pink popper game," he called out.

He stomped in circles. He stomped in figure eights. And he stomped to songs he made up in his head. He stomped until he noticed the plump petals had all been smashed into fragrant oily pulp. Then he scrambled out.

The flowers had been mashed down to less than half the vat full. Now came the chore of filling the rest of the vat with water from the spring. He dragged the heavy bucket to where the stream cascaded off the wall and filled it. He tugged and grunted and slowly dragged it back to the vat. Then he wrestled it to the top of the stairs and poured it into the pulp. It was hard work and he became very tired again. For a while he pretended he was the world's strongest hero, but then even his imagination got tired. One by one, he toted the buckets and poured them in. As the water reached the top, he thought surely now the pool would see that he was no loafer and let the gnomystic dream the way home.

With his job done, Dugan crossed the cavern and found Prompong roasting the rashoo he had captured and popping them greedily into his mouth.

"I'm hungry, too," Dugan said. "You didn't call me to eat."

"You cannot work and eat at the same time," Prompong said with his mouth full.

"Can I eat now?"

"I am finished. You may fire some of what is left."

"When we have company at our house, the guests don't have to cook their own dinner."

Prompong wiped his mouth on his robe.

"You are not company," he said. "You are a problem I must solve."

Dugan picked up the basket, which was now nearly empty from Prompong's over indulgence. Dugan sighed and began to cook his supper over the fire. Prompong had dropped weary weed in the basket so the beetles didn't run out. Dugan was glad he didn't have to chase his dinner again.

"Did you finish your chore?" Prompong said. "Fill it to the top?"

"I did it," Dugan said, "but it was hard work. The buckets were heavy."

Prompong stretched out beside the fire.

"I never carry buckets," he said. "I just slip the chute beneath the waterfall and let it run into the vat."

He pointed to a large bamboo-like stalk cut to work as a pipe. There had been no need to carry heavy buckets of water. There had been no need for all the time it had taken Dugan. He stared angrily at the gnomystic. The little man didn't care how lonely he was for home. He didn't care how frightened and worried Dugan's parents were. Prompong yawned and his one eye strayed with boredom around the walls.

Dugan jumped up, stuck his hands upon his hips and put his very maddest look upon his face. He wanted to yell, but even more, he wanted to go home.

"I did the work. What did your dream tell you?" he asked angrily.

"Dream?" Prompong said. "Oh, yes, my dream. Let me think. Dreams are very difficult to interpret. It takes a trained mind, a keen sense of mysticism. Perhaps I need one more nap."

He rolled over, leaving Dugan to stare at his back.

Dugan plunked back down. He was too tired to argue or to do anything else for that matter. In moments, he too was asleep.

Chapter Seven

The Tunnel

When he awoke, Dugan didn't know how long he'd slept. It could have been hours or it could have been days. In any case, he was hungry. The fire was going and Prompong was threading chestnut-brown fuzzy balls onto a stick and holding them over the fire. When he saw Dugan arise, he pointed toward a shrub where Dugan could pick his own. Dugan silently picked some for himself, then sat down to toast them.

"Qoonots," Prompong said, "not as good as rashoo, but they fill the hallow after a sleep-span and are easier to catch."

Dugan found two qoonots quite filling and quickly finished them. Then hardly daring to hope, he looked Prompong in the face.

"Did you dream?" he asked.

"Dream. Oh mystic dream. Oh powerful dream," Prompong began to singsong.

"Please, just tell me the way out," Dugan said.

Disgruntled, Prompong pursed his lips and then resumed his slow chatter.

"I see a passage. It wanders upward toward a brilliant speck. Something is looking down from the speck. It is a small dark creature that searches for something."

Dugan's eyes brightened.

"It's Dargon," he said. "It's Dargon. He's looking for me."

"Yes, I believe it is so," Prompong said.

"Where? Where? Which way?"

"Oh, Mystic Waters, fulfill my dreams. The way? The way?"

Slowly the shaft began to turn. The mystic turned with it. He turned nearly a full circle, and then back again. Around, then back. Dugan thought it would never halt. Then at last it slowly settled and pointed at one of the many passages that lead from the cavern.

"There," Prompong said.

Dugan did not hesitate a moment. He snapped on his belt, plopped his hat upon his head, filled his pockets with qoonots, his canteen with water, and then raced toward the tunnel and home. At the entry, he paused and looked back.

"Thank you. Thank you," he shouted to Prompong.

He took his first step into the passage. His hopes and spirits flew ahead of him. He would soon be home. He began to run, exhilarated with hope. It didn't bother him that the tunnel was scarcely taller than he and only three times wider. The glowing white stone of the walls gave off a pleasant light and warmth that was almost cheerful. Dugan smiled. He was going home. He was going home!

After a while, his run turned into a fast walk, then a slower walk. There was no change; each step was the same as the last. The vast whiteness stretched forever before and forever behind him. He tried to keep up his cheeriness with the faith that it would not be much longer before he saw sunshine and blue sky and the comfortable homes of his own neighborhood. Still a little color would have been a pleasant diversion.

He began to sing all of his favorite songs to keep himself company. Then he sang them all again. He walked for what seemed a very long time, then sat down to a small lunch of qoonots.

As he ate, he thought about the good food waiting at home. He thought about how his mom smiled while she served it. Chicken.

Potatoes. Gravy. Steak. Apple salad. Chocolate cake. Grape juice. What would be for dinner? Or was it breakfast now? Or perhaps it was the middle of the night and he'd have to wake his parents up. He hoped not. He preferred to imagine he would arrive just in time for dinner.

He finished his qoonots and began to walk again. With his stomach full and his legs rested, he felt more hopeful again and hurried along at the quick pace it usually took to keep up with his dad. Not long after his meal, the tunnel began to taper and grow smaller. The farther he went the smaller it got until he had to crawl upon his hands and knees to fit through the tiny space. Fear began to replace his hopefulness. What would he do if he met something frightful? Something fearsome? He shivered. He hoped the pool knew what it was doing. He crawled as quickly as he could and prayed to his guardian angel to make the way safe.

In the small space the glowing white stone

was a comfort, but it soon came to an end. Now the tunnel was lined with stones that were round and glassy and tightly packed like a can full of marbles. Most were as black as Halloween cats. Others glowed eerily red, blue, green and yellow. It was both magical and spooky. Their glow was barely enough to light the way.

Dugan's stomach filled with willywickers that crept up his spine and caught hold of his breath. But his eyes were filled with magic and enchantment. His imagination flew back and forth between wizard towers and dragon dens. Every feeling he had ever known seemed to jumble together and appear in his mind one after another like messages in the window of a magic eight-ball.

He tried to hurry, but the stones rolled like bearings beneath his hands and legs. Sometimes he went nowhere. Then zing, his hands would fly from beneath him and he would zip along like groceries on a conveyor belt. Mostly he crawled and tried not to think about how much the hard lumps hurt his hands and knees.

After a long while, he stopped, stretched out and propped his chin upon his hands. It seemed a very long time since he had left Prompong and it did not look like the tunnel was going to end any time soon. In fact, it felt like the tunnel ran downhill! Downhill was not the way home. He was tired and lonely again. The tunnel lay darkly ahead and darkly behind. What if the pool was wrong, he thought. Maybe he was going the wrong way. Maybe he should go back. But how could he? He couldn't even turn around. And it was so far back. He had to go on.

As he lay there resting, he studied the bewitching colored stones. They glowed so dimly and yet so beautifully. He stroked his hands over them. They were very smooth and very cool. For a few moments he forgot everything except their enchantment. Like jewels in a pirate's chest, they teased his imagination. He plucked some small ones and rolled them between his fingers. His eyes sparkled and his heart beat faster. In those moments, he knew how it would feel to be a great wizard, to gaze into a crystal ball, and do feats of great magic. There was magic in these stones. He had to take some home.

He popped the little ones into a pocket, and proceeded to pick some more. But a curious thing began to happen. As he plucked the stones, he felt a little breeze stream out of each hole. It was cool upon his face and felt rather refreshing. He picked some more. But with each stone picked, the breeze grew stronger until it grew into a wind. The wind became so strong the stones began to hop out by themselves.

At first there were only a few of them, then more and more gave way. Soon they were popping like popcorn in a popper. They shot in all directions. They bounced off of Dugan. Thump. Thump. The wind grew stronger.

Dugan's hair stood on end. His clothes flapped. The rocks whirled and battered him. His head swam with dizziness. He gripped his hat to protect his head and began to crawl forward as quickly as he could move.

Behind him the crunch of stone hitting stone grew louder and louder as the wind grew stronger and stronger. Like a chain unraveling, the stones popped and popped, foot by foot, collapsing the tunnel into a whirling rage that chased after him. Then suddenly the wind raced up his pant legs and ballooned his jeans. It lifted him slightly and then drove him forward like a rocket. Faster and faster he flew. He dipped and wound and spun through the dark corridor. He could hear the roar and the crash that followed after him only a few feet behind.

He was too frightened to think, and even if he could have, there was nothing he could do but fly with the wind. Then suddenly it was lighter ahead. He shot out of the darkness into a small room lit by the familiar white stones. He landed with a thud upon the dirt floor. The avalanche rumbled behind him. The first stones bounced out after him. He scrambled to his feet.

Dugan leaped to the wall and began to climb up the rocks that jutted out of it. It was not easy. He placed a foot, hugged the wall and pulled with all the might his arms could muster. One step at a time. His fingers clawed the stone. His toes curled up inside his sneakers as though they could grip the meager steps he tried to find footing upon. Beneath him the shooting rocks were beginning to pile up.

Suddenly the stone he stood upon gave way and his foot slid. He clung tightly with both hands as he dropped and dangled there. Loose dirt fell into his face and mouth. Grit filled his teeth. He tried to spit it out while he clung for his life. His feet scraped the wall searching for something to stand upon. Then his left foot found a small hole, just big enough for a sneaker toe. He pushed himself up and found another hole and then a rock. Once more he began to move upward.

While he climbed, the colored stones cannonballed from the tunnel. The cracking of stone pelting stone thundered up the hole and made the walls tremble. His heart was pumping, pumping, driving him upward. His muscles tensed. His only thought was to get high enough fast enough. Then his hand slipped and he teetered backward, certain he was about to fall.

For a moment everything was still, then he felt something soft and warm in his hand. It pulled him gently upward. For a moment he thought he saw a silhouette of shimmering color, like oil upon a pool. Its soft glow filled him with wonder, washing away his fear. His hands and feet seemed to work on their own as he took the last two steps to the safety of a wide ledge, then the warm glow was gone.

From there he watched the stones burst into pieces and fill the hole. Like jewels in a chest, brilliant and bedazzling, they rose until they covered the mouth of the tunnel and sealed it off. Then the clatter was over and only a lonely, spooky silence was left. Now he couldn't go back to Prompong even if he wanted to. He looked around him, hoping to see what had caught his hand and prevented his fall. He felt a twinkle in his heart.

"Thank you, my Angel," he whispered. He closed his eyes a moment. "You don't suppose I could just open my eyes and be home, do you?" he asked. He opened his eyes and sighed. "I didn't think so."

Across from him was the mouth of another tunnel. There was no choice. He worked his way around the ledge until he reached it and stepped inside. It was tall and light. For that much he was grateful. It stretched into the distance without end. But there was still a chance that this was the right path, the one that the pool had directed him to take on his homeward journey. He rinsed the dirt out of his mouth with his canteen, ate his last qoonot, and began his journey again.

His steps were slow and tired. He wished he could know that this was indeed the way. With his head hung low, he walked and walked and walked.

"If I ever get home, I'm never leaving my yard again," he muttered.

After a long and hungry time, the passage came to an end. A wall of rock stood before him, but it had a crack to one side. With both hope and apprehension, he squeezed through the crack, then circled back and forth around a dozen massive stones and came out in a cavern. His eyes roved over the large spacious room. Then his mouth gaped and his heart sank as realization came to him. A few feet away, Prompong sat roasting rashoo. The passages had formed a horseshoe that lead back to the Cavern of the Pool.

Chapter Eight

The Wannaminnihahas

Dugan stomped angrily to where Prompong sat.

"You told me a lie. I walked and walked and almost got killed. The only place I went was back here," he said.

Prompong popped a rashoo into his mouth, licked his fingers, and then picked up another one.

"Prompong does not lie," he said. "If you did not go where you wished to go, it is because you are still not worthy of the Great One's help."

"But I helped you," Dugan said.

"I cannot change what is. Eat and sleep if you must. I will try to think of a more worthy project."

When Dugan awoke, he was alone. He wandered around the cavern until he found Prompong sipping from the vat where he had stomped the flowers.

"I have never seen anyone sleep so much," Prompong said when he saw Dugan.

Dugan heaved a sigh and dropped his head sadly.

"Still I have decided to give you another chance," Prompong said.

"Please," Dugan said. "I can do it."

"I'm not so sure," Prompong said. "This will take courage."

Dugan hesitated, then added less surely, "I have courage."

Prompong sat down and leaned against the vat.

"A ways from here live the most evil of creatures, the Wannaminnihahas. They stole the Eye of the Paramoos, which belongs to the Pool. They have placed it in the eye of their own stone hubba-god. You must take it from there. Then you will find great favor with the Pool when you return it," Prompong said.

"That sounds dangerous," Dugan said.

"I knew my great efforts would be wasted upon you. I have thought my head into ripples of pain for a loafer."

Dugan's lower lip slid out in dismay.

"I'll go," he said.

Prompong pointed him in the direction of his mission.

"But remember, do not let them see you. They are the most evil of creatures. If they catch you, they will tell you lies and fill your mind with such confusion, you will never find your way home. The Pool will not read for you. You will live your days as a lost creature in the bowels of the Down-Under."

Dugan shuddered as he stood and looked

toward the passage that would lead him once more to danger. But what was there for him if he didn't go?

"Angel, my Angel," he whispered, "I think I'm really going to need you this time."

Hesitantly, he took his first few steps. He looked back toward Prompong, hoping he would change his mind, but the weird little man stood resolute. Dugan knew there would be no other choice for him. He reached the mouth of the tunnel and looked far ahead. It was very wide and tall and was well lit by the white stone. Plants grew abundantly as though the stone were their sun. White sand upon the floor made it nearly beach-like. Under other circumstances, Dugan would have liked to play here. But play was not on his mind now.

As he walked, he wondered what the most evil of creatures would look like and how many of them there would be. Fighting a giant peeper and outrunning an avalanche had been scary enough. Could Wannaminnihahas be worse? He shuddered. His only hope would be to sneak up on them without being seen. He thought of trackers and hunters. He thought of Indian braves and Japanese Ninjas. Every now and then he'd whisper to himself, "I'm Dugan the Daring, I can sneak anywhere."

He thought and he walked. While he walked it was often hard to keep his thoughts on the trouble ahead. The walk was much too pleasant. From time to time, he'd stop to peer at some strange plant or odd creature. Sometimes he just stopped to pick up the clean white sand and feel it run through his fingers. How could evil or danger exist in someplace so peaceful and pretty? It was a question there seemed to be no answer for, just as there seemed no answer to many things lately. He sat down to rest and pulled out some tidbits he'd packed for himself back at the cavern. After a brief meal, he fell asleep.

Dugan had no way of knowing how long he

slept. Maybe an hour. Maybe eight hours. There was no time here. Maybe if he stayed here forever he'd never even grow up. He did not like that thought. His favorite wish was to grow up to be his dad's partner. He sighed. Before he could grow up or do anything, he first had to find and outwit the Wannaminnihahas.

He resumed his walk toward the lair of the fearsome beasts and wondered how far he still had to go.

He had not gone far when he came to a beautiful sight. Falls cascaded from the wall. Springs bubble up from the floor. They ran together to form a river. Dugan was delighted. The water was clear and inviting. It was the grandest water park he could imagine. He was most tempted to jump in and play, but he knew he must tend to his mission. Then he could go home where even the sprinkler on the hose would be beautiful.

Dugan walked along close to the river,

peering down into it and sometimes dragging his hands and enjoying the pleasantness of the water. More springs and falls flowed into it as he went along, and the river grew deeper and wider. Beautiful flowers of yellow, coral and purple covered the rocks along the water's edge. Small trees and bushes in hues of copper, green and burgundy created a rainbow forest that was magical to the eyes and mind. Only the sound of the gently flowing water broke the silence. Dugan thought it must be an enchanted land.

It was becoming harder and harder to keep his mind on the reason for his journey. But the farther he went, the more cautious he became, thinking surely he was close to the terrible wicked creatures by now.

Suddenly a loud shriek pierced his ears. It was followed by whoops and hollers and sharp hoo-hoo-hoo's. If it weren't for the loud pounding in his chest, he would have guessed that his heart had dropped into his sneakers. His feet wanted to run and the rest of him wanted to go with them. He scrunched behind a bush, more frightened than he had yet been. "I'm Dugan the Daring," he whispered to himself. "Dugan the Daring." But he didn't feel daring. He trembled at the unknown danger that lay just beyond his sight. Maybe they had already seen him. Maybe the whoops were their alarm and in a moment they would surround him. Maybe he should run now. Maybe if he closed his eyes tight he'd wake up from a bad dream.

He huddled more tightly beneath the bush and listened intently. More whoops and hoo hoo's pierced the underworld, but they did not get any closer. Dugan heard no footsteps or heavy breathing besides his own. After a long while he calmed enough to let a few thoughts creep through his head. What should he do now?

At last he gathered his courage and crawled out on his belly. He sneaked along the river not making a sound. He crept closer and closer toward the shouts and the grimmest mission of his life. His imagination flared with outrageous possibilities.

The river had grown very wide and when it came to a bend, the large passage opened into a sweeping cavern. A glorious array of colors painted rock formations of ribbons and towers, spirals and beams, bridges and stairways. Everywhere plants flourished in odd and interesting shapes. Abundant fruit hung on colossal vines. Flowers in colors he couldn't name spread in carpets upon the floor and across the walls. He caught his breath. He thought it was the most magical place that could possibly exist!

There were no buildings or homes made by the creatures. It seemed nature had merely constructed a park to live in. They could sleep or eat or play wherever they chose. There were nooks for privacy and comfy beds of velvety growth. There were bubbling pools to bathe in and steaming pools to cook in. Everything was as clean and orderly as any mom could wish. Oh how his mom would love this place!

Then his eyes swept back to the river where he saw creatures such as he had never imagined before. They were very human-like and stood on two legs. Their feet had very long toes. A soft gray hair covered their bodies, but it was so short and fine, it almost looked like smooth skin. Enormous bellies hung over bright cloths wrapped around their waists. Their cheeks were quite plump, their noses broad, and their large human-like ears rose to a point. Bushy tufts of curly purple hair stood on top of their heads.

The creatures whooped with glee as they played in the water. Some of the largest ones stood in water up to their waists and rolled their huge bellies. With each roll, the water rose up into waves that washed away into the

distance. Upon these waves, little ones rode on surfing disks. It looked to Dugan to be great fun. The little ones shrieked and laughed and waved their arms. This made the big fat ones laugh harder too. Their bellies rolled harder and the waves grew higher and the little ones laughed with more delight.

Everywhere Dugan looked, the creatures played or ate or lolled beside the river in a most cheerful manner. They could not possibly be the wicked thieves that Prompong had sent him to find, he thought. Perhaps they might even help him on his mission. He had just about made up his mind to step out of hiding when his eyes came to the center of what people would call a town square. There he spied the hubba-god. It was just as Prompong had described it. In the middle of its head sparkled the crystal blue eye he must take and return to the Pool.

Dugan gulped. He began to tremble again. He had never stolen anything before. Stealing was wrong and he could not steal. But he reminded himself that it was not really stealing. They had stolen it from the Pool and he was only returning it to the true owner.

He left his hat, belt and jacket behind the rock and crept out on his belly as quiet as an ant on parade. From rock to rock and bush to bush, he crawled, keeping low, keeping quiet, keeping his eyes and ears alert. He moved slowly to avoid attention. The Wannaminnihahas did not notice him. They were too busy enjoying themselves and having fun.

The hubba-god stood near the river. Dugan quietly slipped into the water. Lucky for Dugan, the river had banks that hung over the water. Bushes and rocks and roots added to the cover. The water was up to his waist. He tucked himself tightly into the recess and moved very slowly so as not to ripple the water.

He passed the first couple who were eating something from a basket that smelled deliciously spicy. Next he passed a happy group who were heartily eating and laughing. Sweet and fruity aromas floated around him and reminded him of his empty stomach. Jolly picnickers lined the riverbank, too busy with their merriment to notice him. Even so, he wondered how they could not hear his heart pounding like jungle drums, the beat growing louder and faster with each step he waded.

When at last he reached the point where he would have to crawl out of the river to reach the hubba-god, there was no one else around. He peered up over the embankment and surveyed the surroundings. This was one place he guessed that someone, if not the creatures themselves, had had a hand in building. A ring of stone pillars separated the hubba-god from the rest of the cavern. Behind the far side of the ring, a stone wall rose nearly to the ceiling. Flowers cascaded down the face and miniature waterfalls sparkled like liquid crystal. This created a magnificent backdrop for the rectangular altar that stood just inside the pillars. Three stairs led up to the highly polished floor, which was a mosaic masterpiece of faces from their past.

It was here the hubba-god stood tall with a look of great importance. It was carved out of rose quartz and struck Dugan with such awe, that for several moments he could only stare in frozen wonderment. He had once visited a cathedral with stained glass windows and beautiful statues that had made him feel this way. He listened for the sound of wings and songs of angels for it was glorious to behold. The radiant Eye of the Paramoos dazzled like a pure blue star.

Dugan's heart pounded worse than ever. He did not steal. He did not want to steal. Even from evil creatures he did not want to steal, but this. . . this felt like church!

He slid out of the water onto his belly and slid behind a pillar. He peeked around, but they were all still occupied with their play outside this special area. He slid across the opening to the next pillar and the next, working his way around the ring, like a snake, he thought, a dirty, crummy snake. This was not a mission for a hero or a knight.

At last he reached the foot of the altar and crept up the stairs snake-like, staying low on his belly. When he reached the beautiful floor, it was polished so brightly he could see his own face among the gentle faces that were honored in this shrine. He did not want to look at his reflection of guilt. He knew he did not belong here. He wanted to whisper to his angel, but he was afraid she would be too angry to listen to him now.

When he reached the hubba-god, he paused with trembling. He could see to great depths in the beautiful rose stone. He did not know if it was real or imagination. Perhaps he was looking into the center of the Earth. Perhaps he was looking into the far universe. Perhaps he was gazing into heaven itself. Perhaps it was the greatest magic he had ever seen. If kindness had an image, he was looking into its face. He wanted to slide back across the floor and sit at a respectful distance where he could gaze with good feelings and tell his angel how he felt.

His heart ripped apart in his small chest. This was his only way home. Prompong and the Pool had told him these were thieves and the Eye was not theirs. Hair was standing up on the back of his neck and his throat was as dry as rawhide. Maybe it was all a spell, he thought and once he had the Eye he could see how evil these creatures were. Maybe the beauty would vanish and his angel would be happy he had saved the Eye and returned it to the Pool where it belonged.

Very hesitantly, he placed his hand upon the stone god. It was cool and smooth. He placed a foot into the carved folds of its draped robe. He found a ridge to grip and another foothold and began to move upward. Slowly and silently he maneuvered up the garment and into the cradle of the god's arms where he crouched. Then he paused and looked around. Everyone was still busy. Laughter, the splash of waves, the whoops of young ones and the chatter of friends filled the air. But Dugan trembled in terror.

He slowly rose and worked his way up and onto the shoulder. From here he could stand and reach the Eye. Here he stood eye to dazzling Eye. It sparkled brilliantly, like an eternal flame, a blue gleam in the eye of heaven, a mystery of the Universe. His breath stuck in his throat. How could he touch it? It was as though God Himself were watching. Was that his angel tugging at his pant leg, begging him to climb down? His hand moved slowly toward the Eye.

"Stop, Thief!" a thunderous voice commanded.

His body went limp. He dizzied with fright. He looked down and knew there was no escape. At the bottom of the statue stood the two biggest Wannaminnihahas and they weren't laughing now. Even Mrs. Murphy hadn't looked this angry. Beyond them, the others had stopped their frivolities. They stared sternly at him. Then everyone rose at once and moved toward him.

"Come down, Thief," the same voice said harshly.

Dugan shook so badly his feet couldn't find the footing to climb down. He hugged the god and half slid, half fell into the grasp of his captors.

"You dare to steal from the Wannaminnihahas?!" said King Hoagy-Hoagy.

Dugan's eyes were wide with fright. His lips trembled and words would not come out.

"Where do you come from?" the king thundered.

"The. . . the. . . Great Out-There," Dugan stammered.

"You come into our world to steal?!"

"I only wanted to take the Eye back to the Pool where it belongs. You're the ones who stole it."

"The Wannaminnihahas do not steal. Who tells such lies?"

"Prompong told me," Dugan said.

Dugan hung his head. A tear ran down his cheek.

"I did not want to steal anything. I am lost. I want to go home. Prompong said the Pool wouldn't tell me the way out unless I got its Eye back."

The king studied him thoughtfully and made a sign to the two who held him. His captors loosened their grip and set him down next to King Hoagy-Hoagy.

"A glass of jolliwoll," the king ordered.

A very gentle looking female handed Dugan a glossy black stone hollowed out for a glass. Into it she poured a clear red liquid that fizzled and tickled his nose. Was this the way they got rid of thieves? His stomach somersaulted with dread. Would one quick gulp mean he'd never see home again?

"Drink," the king ordered.

Slowly, Dugan obeyed.

It was very good. Even better than cherry cola and so fizzy it made him want to laugh. In fact, he would have laughed if he had not been so scared. But the moments passed and he felt no worse.

"I think perhaps you were tricked," said the king. "You do not look like a thief."

"I'm not," Dugan said. "I promise, I'm not."

Suddenly he fell silent. He remembered one of the last things his mother had said to him was that his promises were no good. Would the king also think his promises were no good?

"Tell King Hoagy-Hoagy your story, then I will decide what is to be done with you."

A glass of jolliwol was filled for the king and Dugan's glass was refilled. The Wannaminnihahas gathered closer to hear his sad tale.

When he finished, the king leaned back and studied him carefully.

"It was a bad thing you tried, this stealing," he said.

"I know," Dugan said and hung his head shamefully. "I'm sorry. I just wanted to go home."

"If I knew the way, I would help you."

"The Pool… "

The Pool of the Seven Unvirtues tells nothing but one's sins," the king said. "Did you not notice the strange creatures that are trapped there?"

"They were strange all right."

"Did Prompong ever go near the water?"

"Never."

"You must learn about the Pool," the king said. "The good have nothing to fear. If they fall in, they will float and save themselves. The bad will sink to their most ungodly level and take the form of their bad deeds."

Dugan's eyes grew larger as he remembered how close to the edge he had walked. He had even thought of swimming in it.

"At the top the yellow cowards fearfully tremble and dash about, afraid to drop their guard for even a moment. Most disconcerting for a creature of peace. Beneath them are the unclean, those who did not honor the gift of their bodies with proper care. Their bodies are black crusted and the water turns dark wherever they go."

"Hey, my mom says 'Cleanliness is next to Godliness,' Dugan said.

"I think I would like this mom," said the king, and then continued. "The third layer holds the cheaters. Their bellies bulge from the weight of what they cheated away from others. Their bulging eyes forever dart about in search of what is not theirs."

"I saw those," Dugan said. "They were ugly."

"The deeper, the uglier," the king said. "The fourth layer is for liars and gossips. Barbed tongues wag from their big ugly mouths. The mouths they used to hurt and deceive others now prick their own bodies and cause themselves the pain they caused others."

Dugan gulped. He never meant to lie. But sometimes he forgot to keep his promises. Maybe he would have to try harder.

The king continued. "Next the greedy and the selfish are puffed to enormous size and wear heavy gaudy scales. These scales are the weight of taking too much for the self and having too little care for fellow creatures."

"I'm not selfish," Dugan said enthusiastically. "I share."

"That is good. We also share. It is part of our secret to happiness."

"What's next?"

King Hoagy-Hoagy paused and looked Dugan directly in the eyes.

"The thief," he said. "They are made up of parts stolen from life's most unfavorite creatures. Parts from snakes and bats and other hated things. Each time a creature steals from another, he also robs himself of a piece of his own beauty."

"I'll never be a thief again," Dugan said. "I promise."

King Hoagy-Hoagy watched Dugan cross his heart. Then the king placed the tip of his long velvety finger upon the spot Dugan crossed.

"What did that heart feel when you climbed the hubba-god?" the king asked.

"I felt I was doing something really terribly wrong and very bad. I thought my angel might go away."

"But you did not listen to your heart."

"Prompong told me you were evil and you had stolen the Eye first."

"What did your heart tell you?"

"That you must be kind and good to live so happy and have so much fun together."

"But you listened to Prompong instead of your heart. Did you not trust your own heart?"

"I needed to go home. I thought that was the way."

"What do you think now?"

"Maybe I should have listened to my heart. Maybe it's my good detector."

King Hoagy-Hoagy smiled.

"Hearts are often wise long before heads," he said.

The Wannaminnehahas around him smiled and nodded in agreement.

The king continued. "At the very bottom of the Pool lie the worst of all, the cruel and destructive. They are separated from all others forever by the barbs and blades that tear apart anything that they touch. They must be vigilant all the time so that one of their own kind does not run into them. The most painful part of this is that they cannot draw close to another creature for comfort."

"Wow, I hope I never fall in," Dugan said.

A basket of food was placed between them. The king handed Dugan a soft yellow pod. Dugan broke it open and sucked berry-like pulp from inside.

"Why is one so young, so fearful?" asked the king.

Dugan lowered his eyes sadly.

"Well, for one thing, I promised my mother I wouldn't leave my yard. In fact, I promised her that a lot, and I broke my promises," Dugan said. "That's almost like lying. I didn't mean to."

"I see," said the king. "Promises are very important."

"I know," Dugan said.

He glanced toward the hubba-god.

"Why does the hubba-god feel so good... like heaven?" Dugan asked.

King Hoagy-Hoagy smiled.

"Of course, it is not really a god. It is a beautiful place to sit and think beautiful thoughts of kindness and love. Those feelings have all been captured in the radiant stone we call our hubba god. We need only think of someone, even our ancestors, to feel their love.

Since the Grand Creator set us in this place, all Wannaminnihahas have added their heart feelings here. That is why we are so happy."

"Wow, that's magic," Dugan said and stared in awe at the wondrous altar.

"It is the Grandest Magic. Heart Magic," said King Hoagy-Hoagy.

All the other Wannaminihahas had remained in respectful silence while their king spoke with Dugan. Then as last there were a few giggles here and there. Dugan glanced around at the kindly faces. Their cheerfulness was returning. Most of them were even smiling.

"Does everyone in the Out-There have such hair?" one asked with a curious giggle.

Dugan touched his sandy hair, blushed, and recited the colors of human hair.

"I have not seen such wrappings?" said another.

Dugan looked down at his jeans and tee shirt and remembered his jacket and belt behind the bush. Then he looked at their colorful wrap cloths. There was no need for pockets or tool belts in the wonderland they lived in.

"You are very different than us," said another, "but I like you anyway. There is pleasantness about you."

"I like you, too," Dugan said. "I wanted to play with you when I first saw you, but I was afraid."

"I have decided," King Hoagy-Hoagy said loudly, "that we are glad you came. We forgive you."

The others hooted and cheered their approval. Dugan grinned until his cheeks ached.

For a while Dugan let his fears and worries rest. The kind and happy creatures traded stories with him and laughed with delight when he described the Great Out-There. Their eyes glowed with warmth when he told them about his mom and dad and Dargon. Dugan beamed when they expressed their admiration for Mr. And Mrs. Peckles.

His kindly hosts brought him more good things to eat and drink. He rode the river waves with the little ones and laughed and played until he could hardly move. Then tired, but happy, he lay down to rest upon a soft violet mat that nature had woven.

When he awoke, he found the others sitting quietly within the ring around the altar. They breathed gently and wore soft smiles upon their faces. Their bodies relaxed in restful peace. When the king saw Dugan had awakened, he rose and others followed him. They brought baskets of food and set them around Dugan.

"I should go now," Dugan said.

The king nodded.

"We know," he said.

Tears glistened in Dugan's eyes.

"Can't anyone help me?" he asked.

"You are welcome to stay with us. But we do not know the way to the Out-There. The world we love is here and we do not stray far."

Dugan wiped his face on his sleeve.

"I like you," he said. "I like all of you. But I miss my mom and dad. They're worried about me. I have to find a way home."

"You have courage," said the king. "We will pray for the Light to show you the way. Eat your fill, then take all you can carry so that you may eat for strength on your journey. Think of us as the fruits part your lips. Our hearts will follow you to steady you on your way."

Dugan thanked and hugged King Hoagy-Hoagy and those closest to him. Then he picked up a full basket, waved good-bye to the others and set off back the way he had come, headed for the Cavern of the Pool.

Chapter Nine

On His Way

It seemed a long ways back, but his mind was full of thoughts as he plodded along. He was once again without help or a plan. He was on his own now. Although the outlook was grim, his heart still carried a buoyancy from the time he had spent with the Wannaminihahas. Though he had left them behind and would never see them again, somehow he felt they weren't far away. He remembered one of the last things King Hoagy-Hoagy had said was, "We

will pray for the Light to show you the way."
Dugan believed the Light would listen to the
kind creatures. If only King Hoagy-Hoagy
could meet his mom and dad.

After he had trekked a very long time, he
crawled beneath a shrub and fell into a deep
sleep. When he awoke, he did not go far before
he recognized the opening of the Cavern of the
Pool. Tingles ran through him. What would he
say to Prompong?

He found the gnomystic lounging in a
cozy nook. One eye watched a hairy gray bug
upon a yellow pod while the other eye
wandered around in its usual bored manner.
When Dugan stepped in front of him, he
was so surprised, the wandering eye snapped
back in line with the other and stared
anxiously at Dugan.

"You have returned!" Prompong said.

Dugan stood silent.

Prompong leaped to his feet.

"You have brought me the Eye of the Paramoos?" he said.

"No," Dugan said. "They caught me."

Prompong's eyes widened.

"But you are back."

"They let me go. They said the Eye is not yours."

Prompong began to stomp and rant.

"You let them fool you! Did I not tell you they were the most evil of creatures? Did you not know they would lie?"

"They were nice to me," Dugan said.

"That is part of their treachery. Foolish child! Unworthy child! The Pool will not forget!"

Dugan backed away, fearful of the gnomystic's rage, but Prompong would not let him get away. Dugan continued to back up and back up, but Prompong followed with both eyes focused tightly upon his face. He tore at his beard and tugged at his robe of peeper wrappings.

"The great Pool asks a small favor of you and you let those sneaky creatures fool you!?"

Dugan backed up more rapidly. Prompong's rage was beginning to frighten him. He forgot everything around him except the snarling face that charged him and grew more angry by the moment. In his hurry to get away, he did not realize that he was backing straight for the Pool itself, nor did Prompong. Like tango partners bent together toward the final dip, Prompong leaned menacingly closer, following Dugan's every step. Closer and closer to the Pool of the Seven Unvirtues.

"Curses! Curses!" Prompong shouted.

Then he lunged full force toward Dugan with his hands outstretched to catch him by the throat. Dugan leaped to the side to dodge the attack. Then they both saw the Pool, but it was too late for Prompong. He tried to catch his footing at the edge, but the windings of his robe had fallen loose from his tugging them in a tantrum. His foot hung in the folds.

Prompong tumbled headlong into the water. Dugan watched with great astonishment as Prompong changed into the yellow darting coward, then continued to change through each layer. His eyes bulged like the cheater. His mouth grew large and ugly like the liar. He puffed up with greed until Dugan thought he would burst. Down. Down he sank. He grew barbs and bat wings and razored fins. His skin crusted and scaled. At last, he settled at the bottom, ugliest of the cruel and dishonest.

Dugan stared wide-eyed and backed away. He turned and ran. He barely paused to snatch up his basket of food. Which way to go?

There was nothing to show him one passage was better than another. He hesitated only briefly, then headed for the closest exit and ventured into it.

The passage was large enough to walk

through comfortably and the familiar white rocks lit the way. Most of the plants and bugs were now also familiar to him. It now seemed like he had spent half of his life here.

It was strange and sad to be alone again without direction. What if he never got home? What if he was going farther and farther in the wrong direction? What if he was going deeper into the Earth? He stopped and looked back. He could still find his way back to the Wannaminnihahas. He would be safe with them. He looked at his basket. Their food was good. They had lots of fun. He stared back down the tunnel a moment longer, then turned and headed on his journey. No matter what happened, he had to at least try to get home.

After what seemed like a very long time, he sat down beside a small spring that trickled from the wall, took a drink and refilled his canteen. He ate a small portion from his basket. Then he set out again.

Luck for Dugan was a roller coaster. It was up. It was down. It was up. And now it was beginning to go down again. The passage did not continue as an easy course. He soon came to a place where the tunnel narrowed into a slit that he had to slide through sideways. It widened again, then shrank to a crawl space. He got down on his knees and held his basket in his teeth. He could touch both walls with his elbows. The floor ran uphill and down, over piles of rocks, through small ponds and sometimes shrank to belly crawl space.

Then once again, the white rocks ended and he missed their warm glow. Here and there a pale yellow stone glowed dull and dingy like a dirty bug light. The light was stingy and unfriendly as if it would rather not glow at all. Dugan's spirits dropped lower. Remembering the giant peeper, he again became fearful of what might lurk behind the next rock or upon the next ledge or in the next puddle.

The difficult trek made him very tired and he wondered where he would sleep next. He did not like to think of sleeping alone in the gloomy, twisted tunnel.

Then the passage narrowed into a wide crack in a large gray rock. Maybe it was the end, he thought. He squeezed through to see if there was something on the other side. Much to his surprise, he stepped out into a cavern of enormous size, even larger than the Cavern of the Pool.

It was not as pleasant though. It was not bright and flat and open. It was lit by the dull yellow stones that tossed their light as half-heartedly as Dugan felt. A small stream ran through it. Large boulders and small valleys were scattered throughout it. The walls were full of nooks and crannies where a thousand creepy things could hide. Vines hung down from the ceiling and the walls. Plants that grew upon the walls were unpleasant shades of brown and mustard.

Dugan plopped down. He was too tired to explore and too tired to worry about the safety of lying down. He found a niche between two rocks where a mossy growth made a soft bed, and quickly fell asleep.

Chapter Ten

Oscat

Dugan awoke to a silence and loneliness that made him so sad he did not want to get up. He did not know if it was night or day. He missed the brightness of the sun and the sounds of the world at home. Sounds like Dad humming while he shaved. Dargon panting. Mom clattering pans and dishes. Toast popping. And most of all, the voices of people he loved and trusted.

He sat and sat, too discouraged to move. He

had no idea which way to try next. For all he knew this could be the center of the Earth. But at last the boredom of sitting overcame his reluctance to move and he rose and began to wander around the enormous room. Dugan just could not sit still for very long no matter what. He had to make up his mind and head in a new direction. He slowly turned in a full circle.

"Eeny, meeny, miny, moe. Which way would a sunflower grow?"

Suddenly a shriek cut the silence and pierced Dugan with fright. He trembled from head to toe. Another shriek followed. He turned toward it, and then took a giant leap backwards. Only a few feet from him slithered the ugliest black thing he had ever seen. It looked like a large chunk of raw liver with horrid green eyes. It slid over the rocks and through the crevices more like a snake than an animal. It was chasing and about to catch something just out of Dugan's sight. Then he saw the flick of a wing. He grabbed a rock and let out a shout that echoed throughout the large cavern. The rock missed the wretched creature, but bounced close enough to give it a good scare. The green eyes doubled in size and changed to liquid purple as it stared in surprise at Dugan. Then it quickly slithered away, plopped into a stream and disappeared.

Dugan hastened to the creature he had saved. It was hidden in a cluster of rocks. Dugan slipped up quietly and peered over a large stone. He saw a small fuzzy copper cat-like tail that drooped sadly on the ground. Only the tip flicked slightly from time to time. He leaned a little farther over until he could see the back end of something very much like the baby tigers he had seen at the zoo. A blend of burnished brown spots and stripes contrasted its fuzzy soft body of marbled gold and copper.

Then the animal took two steps backwards and as it did, a golden wing unfolded from its body. Dugan stared in wonder for the wing was both surprising and marvelous. It was like a feathered sunset with peacock eyes. Wispy little feelers waved from the tip. Each time the wing folded and opened, it was as magical as opening a treasure chest. Then Dugan noticed that the other wing hung limp as though it was broken. His heart stopped for a moment in dismay that so lovely a creature should be wounded. His first thought was he should take it home for Mom to mend.

Before he could recall that he could not get home to mend anything, the creature turned and faced him. Bright round flame-blue eyes stared at him from the enchanting face of a tiny owl. Gold feathers trimmed in silver decorated the breast of his body. When it fanned its one good wing, Dugan thought it was the most beautiful thing he had ever seen.

"You're an. . . an. . . owl-cat," Dugan said softly and sat very still, captured by its magical beauty.

"I'm called O-scat," the owl-cat said.

For a moment they just stared at each other. Then, all at once they were both hit with the same realization and exclaimed in unison, "You can talk!"

"Of course, I can talk," Dugan said. "I'm a human boy. We all talk. But you're not supposed to talk. But I don't know why I said that. Everything down here talks."

Dugan moved to climb over the rock and Oscat backed up, keeping a fixed eye upon him.

"Don't be afraid," Dugan said. "I won't hurt you. I just want to see your wing."

Oscat looked down at the heap of feathers that hung helpless at his side. A tear rolled down his small cheek. Dugan gently picked him up and supported the injured wing very carefully.

"You're keen," he said, "but you're so small."

"I'm not very old," Oscat said. "I don't even know how to fly yet."

Dugan looked around nervously. Where there

was a baby anything, there was a mother close by. He knew from his own mom how fierce one could be if she was worried about her offspring.

"What are you looking for?" Oscat asked.

"Your mother," Dugan replied.

"She left and never came back," Oscat said. "Maybe she didn't like me."

Dugan sat down and cuddled the little owl-cat to his chest. He began to cry, too.

"I can't find my mother either," he said. "But it's because I got lost down here, not because I don't love her. So maybe your mom got lost like me and somewhere she's sad that she can't find you."

Oscat nuzzled his head against Dugan.

"I didn't think of that," he said and the sobbing grew louder. "I'll never be able to fly with this wing. I can't even look for her. I got so hungry up on the ledge, I fell off trying to teach myself to fly."

Dugan stopped crying. Oscat was the saddest

thing he had ever seen. Very carefully, he carried him back to his basket of food and held a tidbit up to the small beak. Oscat did not hesitate. He did not care what it was; it was food.

At last he'd had his fill. Now that he was no longer worried about his stomach, he began to worry about his wing again.

"Maybe I could fix it," Dugan said.

He dug into the pouch on his belt that held his first aid kit. He pulled out a bundle of flat splint sticks and a bandage roll. He had long anticipated having to mend a squirrel or bird or other small animal, because that was what heroes did. His dad had used twigs to show him how to splint a broken bone. But until now he had only put a splint on a rubber doll.

Oscat blinked his eyes and looked hopefully at Dugan. Dugan worked carefully, doing his best to set it just right, but it wasn't as easy as tying up a rubber leg. Whatever he tried, the feathers got in the way. But at last when the wing was bound, Dugan was very proud of his first rescue mission. He could hardly wait to tell his dad what he had done.

"You will get better now," he said, with the air of confidence his mother always used.

Oscat stared at Dugan's work. His wing looked very odd, but it felt better. There was something about Dugan that made him believe maybe everything was going to be all right after all. Dugan sat down next to his little patient. Oscat stretched out and laid his head on Dugan's knee.

"Do you know how to get to the Great Out-There?" Dugan asked.

"I only know what I could see from my ledge," Oscat said.

"I didn't think you could help, but it was nice to meet you anyway."

Dugan latched up his first-aid kit.

"I have to get going," he said.

"Leave me?" Oscat said. "Who's going to take this thing off of my wing?"

"I don't know," Dugan said, suddenly realizing this really was a problem. "It will take a long time for your wing to get well. And I have to go home."

Oscat began to sob again. "I'll die if you go. Doesn't anyone care about me?"

Dugan thought a moment.

"I'll take you with me," he said.

"I can't go," Oscat said. "I have to be here when my mother gets back. And she told me I must never go to the Out-There."

"Oh brother!" Dugan said.

The little owl-cat looked so sad, Dugan could hardly bear to look at him. He wanted badly to get home as soon as possible. He knew Oscat would die if he left him. And he knew how much Oscat and his mother would want to be together again. For a while he sat very quietly.

"What are you doing?" Oscat finally asked.

"I'm praying."

"Will it help?"

"I sure hope so. All these questions are too hard for a little kid."

Time passed slowly in the cavern. Dugan fed Oscat and cared for his wing. Oscat told Dugan the good things to eat and where to find them as his mother had told him. Soon he started to look healthier and he did not cry as often. He grew at an amazingly rapid rate and ate more than Dugan believed possible for something so small.

When he wasn't eating, Oscat liked for Dugan to stroke him and bathe him and tell him stories about life in the Out-There.

"That doesn't sound so bad," Oscat said on one occasion.

"What do you mean?" Dugan asked.

"Mother said if I ever ventured there, Men would kill me."

Dugan thought about space movies and monster movies he had seen. It was true. People always wanted to hurt things that were different, even before they had a chance to know if they were good or not. Sometimes people even hurt other people who were different. There was a dull ache in his chest to think someone would hurt Oscat and never find out what a gentle friend he was.

"She's probably right," Dugan said sadly.

When Oscat grew stronger, they began to play games. Dugan taught him Hide and Seek. That was Oscat's favorite, but he never liked Dugan to hide too long.

As time passed, Dugan worried more and more. At least a dozen times he almost left. Then he would look at Oscat with his bandaged wing and he couldn't abandon him. He had come to love Oscat and Oscat needed him.

The time finally came when the wing seemed strong enough. Dugan took off the splint and the bandage. The wing was a little stiff and the feathers a bit mussed, but Dugan had done a good job. The bone had mended well. First Oscat moved it carefully, just a bit. A sparkle came into his eyes. He fanned it a little more and then flapped it joyfully. His eyes shone like a dazzling blue flame. He nuzzled his head against Dugan in thanks.

Dugan was glad the wing was healed and he would be able to leave. Oscat had also grown so quickly that he was now half Dugan's size. But now that it was nearly time to say goodbye, Dugan's heart was heavy. A boy didn't find an owl-cat every day, and he knew he'd never see Oscat again. He would also have to leave another comforting friendship and brave the tunnels alone. Reluctantly he began to gather food for his basket.

"What are you doing?" Oscat asked.

"I have to go now," Dugan said.

"But Dugan, I can't learn to fly by myself."

Dugan had not thought of this. Now he was more troubled than ever. He didn't know anything about teaching an owl-cat to fly and he had already been gone from home much too long.

"Oscat, I have to go home," he said.

"But you can't leave me now," Oscat said. "What will I do?"

Oscat crept closer. He laid his head upon Dugan's foot and looked up pleadingly.

"Well, maybe just a little bit longer," Dugan said.

Chapter Eleven

Flying Lessons

Now that his wing was mended, Oscat began to catch bugs for himself and chase other small creatures around the cavern. There were more of the ugly black sliders Dugan had chased off just before their first meeting. There were gray hairless beasts with wrinkled skin and snarled up snouts, and other odd and ugly creatures that Dugan avoided. The only ones Dugan liked were the ones he called sweepers. They were so short and their burnt-orange hair so long, they looked like dust mops scooting across the ground. But the bigger Oscat got, the fewer creatures they saw.

Despite everything else, Dugan had fun. He quickly learned that, like Tarzan, he could swing upon the sturdy vines that hung from the ceiling and walls. It was grand. He'd flap one arm and shout, "Look, Oscat, I can fly."

With Oscat healed, there was less time to play. Dugan had to get serious and teach Oscat to fly. He would send Oscat to the top of a tall rock and call for him to flap his wings and jump. Having tiger back legs made Oscat a good jumper. But when it came to flying, Oscat was not a quick learner. Perched upon a rock he would get so excited about leaping, he would forget to flap. If the rock Dugan sent him to was too tall, he'd apologize to Dugan and climb back down to a rock he was not afraid to leap from. The fall from the ledge as a baby had left him afraid of heights.

Dugan was beginning to understand why his own mother was sometimes frustrated. Being a parent wasn't easy.

Then Dugan got a wonderful idea. He set Oscat upon a tall rock, then tied a vine around his middle and gave him a shove. Back and forth Oscat swung, but he forgot to flap his wings. He closed his eyes and used his wings to cover them.

"Dugan, I think I'm going to be sick," he said.

Dugan helped him down.

"How are you going to learn to fly if it makes you sick? And you can't fly with your eyes closed."

"I know, Dugan," Oscat said, "but it's so scary up there."

He hung his head shamefully.

"That's okay," Dugan said and stroked his head. "I get scared sometimes, too."

"Really, Dugan?"

"My dad told me even he gets scared

sometimes. But he said everything has an answer and when we find the answer, we don't have to be scared anymore."

"I didn't know scared had answers."

Oscat pondered the idea for a moment, then spied a small mole-like creature scampering across the ground.

"Can we eat now?" he asked, already on his way to pounce upon his dinner.

Dugan took his basket to fill it with lunch he didn't have to catch. When Oscat wanted to eat, nothing got into his head that did not gratify his stomach. Dugan ate quietly while he watched his friend bound around the cavern happily pursuing his meal.

When Oscat was finally full, they went back to leaping off rocks in an attempt to build Oscat's courage. Oscat loved Dugan and wanted to please him, but every time he thought about flying, his knees trembled and his wings curled up beneath him. Dugan pleaded with him.

"You've got to try."

Slowly Oscat climbed up upon a tall rock.

"Ok, Dugan. I'll try," he said, reluctantly.

Dugan tied a vine securely around him and shoved him off, but Oscat failed to flap his wings again. Once more, he used them to hide his eyes. Dugan had to do something or he'd never get home. He grabbed a vine for himself, tied it around his waist and swung past his friend.

"Hey, look at me," he called.

Dugan twitched his nose, then crossed his eyes. Oscat giggled. Dugan laughed and twisted his mouth into another silly face as he sailed past. Oscat opened his wings a little. He loved it when Dugan clowned around. He tried to cross his eyes and twist his beak to be like Dugan. Dugan flapped one arm and made monkey noises. Oscat imitated Dugan and tried to flap one wing. Dugan cheered and swung higher. Oscat had to stay close to Dugan so he wouldn't miss a single silly face. Without thinking, he swung higher, too. Dugan flapped one arm and then the other. Without even knowing it, Oscat was soon flapping both wings at the same time. He was having too much fun to remember he was scared.

They clowned around and swung until they had to drop to the ground in joyous exhaustion and fell asleep side by side.

When Dugan awoke, Oscat was already romping around the cavern chasing down his next meal. He ate more and more all the time and seemed to grow before Dugan's eyes.

As soon as they had both eaten, they returned to their flight lessons, which Oscat now thought of as great fun and games instead of the scary job of flying. Dugan tied a vine around Oscat, who did not even wait for Dugan to push him off a ledge. He sailed across the room on his own. Dugan tied himself to a vine and swung out making funny noises like a jet taking off. He swept past Oscat, narrowly missing him. Oscat covered his eyes with his wings and played at being frightened. Dugan howled with laughter and swung higher.

"Oscat can't catch me. I'm a fighter pilot," he shouted.

Oscat wriggled and flapped his wings and tried to catch up with Dugan.

"Oscat can't catch me. Oscat can't catch me," Dugan called as he passed by again and sailed higher.

Oscat flapped harder.

"Nothing outflies an owl-cat," Oscat said, wanting to be a part of the fun.

Up swung his vine, but instead of coming down again, the vine went slack. Oscat soared higher and higher all the way to the ceiling. Dugan was far below. He stared up in surprise.

"Oscat, you're flying," he shouted.

Oscat looked surprised, too. He made two more circles, then swooped down and landed beside Dugan who now stood upon the ground watching in wonder. Dugan untied Oscat's vine and gave his neck a hug. Then with a mighty bound into the air, Oscat took off. He whooshed around the walls and dive-bombed sweepers. He hovered near the ceiling. He landed on his old ledge. Finally he landed beside Dugan again.

"You were great!" Dugan said.

Oscat beamed.

"I'd never have done it without you," Oscat said.

Dugan gave Oscat his biggest hug.

"You know I have to get ready to leave now," Dugan said.

Oscat sat in silence.

"You're not a baby anymore," Dugan said. "You're nearly as big as me."

They sat quietly together for a few moments, then for a time resumed their play. Dugan swung on the vines and Oscat flew until they were hungry and tired. Then they had their meals and fell asleep close beside each other.

Chapter Twelve

The Last Chance

When Dugan awoke, Oscat was gone. Dugan looked across the whole cavern. He thought Oscat would be hunting breakfast, but he wasn't. He thought Oscat would be practicing flying, but he wasn't in the air. Then he thought Oscat must be playing hide and seek. He searched everywhere and still didn't find him. By that time, Dugan was hungry. He gathered his lunch and ate alone. Still no Oscat. He swung on the vines for a while, but it was not fun alone. Finally, he just sat down and waited. He waited and waited. Still no Oscat.

He had planned to leave by now, but he just couldn't leave without saying good-bye. He took a nap and ate again and continued to wait. He began to worry that something had happened to Oscat, and he was angry that Oscat had left him alone. He couldn't think why his friend had deserted him.

At last, the time came when he decided he could wait no longer. He didn't know where to look for Oscat and he had to look for home again. Very sadly, he chose a passage to leave by, then took a last look around him.

"Good-bye, Oscat, wherever you are," he said.

He collected his courage and stepped into the tunnel he had chosen. It was neither large or encouraging or well lit. This time he was lonelier than ever before.

He wandered a long time. Sometimes he walked. Sometimes he crawled. Sometimes he squeezed through the tiniest spaces. He rested and ate, and walked some more. He never knew if he was heading upward or deeper into the Earth. The only thing he knew was that he had to keep going. He had to keep trying although now his spirits were the lowest they had been since he had arrived so long ago.

When he was finally so tired, he didn't think he could take another step, he took a last step out of the tunnel into a cavern. He paused and stared, then dropped onto the nearest rock. He had circled back to the cavern where he had lived with Oscat. But a quick search and a pleading shout told him Oscat had not returned.

Dugan rested. Twice more, he tried to leave. Twice more he ended up back in the cavern, each tunnel a horseshoe, Each time he became sadder and more angry.

"Oscat!" he shouted.

"Oscat. Oscat," the echo called.

"Oscat. Darn you! Why'd you leave me alone?"

The desperation was becoming more than he could bear.

He fell asleep, for how long he couldn't guess. He awoke to a strange noise. He opened his eyes and there before him sat a huge magnificent owl-cat who stared directly at him. Dugan was terrified. It was as large as a full-grown tiger. Its wings spread like a small plane. Dugan tried to back away.

"Dugan," it said. "What's the matter?"

"Oscat?" Dugan asked.

"Of course. Who else?"

"But you're so big!"

Oscat looked down at himself.

"Yeah, I grew a bit," he said. "That's what slowed me down. Growing and eating took a lot of time. That's the way owl-cats are my mom told me. We get to a certain age then suddenly grow and grow until we can't grow anymore. It's very strange to grow so fast. I don't think my brain has caught up."

"Why'd you leave me alone?" Dugan asked with a wounded heart.

"Why, I went to look for the Out-There, of course," Oscat said. "Didn't you know?"

Dugan threw his arms around Oscat's now big neck.

"I've been so lonely," he said, "and I missed you so much."

"I missed you, too," Oscat said. "But it's time for you to go home. And I have to find out what happened to my own mother. Climb onto my back."

"But, Oscat, you can't go to the Out-There. It's too dangerous for you."

"You're my friend, Dugan. You stayed when I needed you. You helped me in every way you could. You taught me to fly and not be afraid. It's my turn to help you."

Dugan gave him another hug, and then climbed upon the feline back. This time he was really going home. Up they rose with a magnificent bound. Oscat was now a splendid flyer. He was powerful and swift. Higher and higher they flew, up to the ceiling, then out through a hole at the top. They sailed through one tunnel, and then another. Oscat swooped and turned and maneuvered like a fighter plane. No one would have guessed how small and frightened he was when Dugan found him. Dugan was so proud. It was a ride he would remember forever.

In his excitement, he almost wished the ride would never end. But then he felt the clean fresh air and saw the break in the rocks and he knew the end was near. He hugged the back of his friend, trying to say with his arms all the things that he felt in his heart. Then they sailed out through the side of the bluffs that towered over one end of his town. It was night. The stars were beautiful. The moon was so big and gold a pirate could mistake it for treasure.

Oscat circled lower and lower toward the ground. When they were quite near, he lowered his tail and hindquarters. Dugan slid from his back onto a pile of autumn leaves. Without stopping, Oscat swooped upwards. Dugan watched as he rose into the night sky, grand and majestic. From Oscat's wings showered bits of the weary weed, which had collected in the feathers when he brushed the walls. It fluttered down and settled upon Dugan's head and shoulders. The last thing Dugan remembered as he drifted away was the magical vision of the magnificent Oscat as he passed before the harvest moon.

"Goodbye, Oscat, my friend," he whispered.

"What?" his mother said, reaching to embrace her son with tears of relief in her eyes. Worry, joy and love filled her voice, "Dugan, where have you been?"

He awoke at his own door in the arms of a big farmer who had found him in the field. He put his arms around his mother's neck and smiled at his father who stood beside her.

"On an adventure," he said, "the spookiest, grandest adventure."

Watch for more Dugan
Adventures coming soon.

#2
Dugan Peckles
and the
Keepers of the
Crystal Flame